"The best is yet to come, Liv."

Zane took a step closer to her. "I hope I can be part of that," he said softly.

Liv's pulse ticked. He was so close that she could smell the cologne he wore and see the golden specks in his brown eyes. Was he offering her a chance to rekindle their relationship? She had never wanted him to kiss her as much as she did in this moment—yet a niggle of doubt pricked her conscience.

Nothing had changed. He was still her daughter Miley's dad, and if she did something to hurt her relationship with him, it would affect her relationship with Miley. It was too soon—and too tender—to risk such a thing.

Liv took a step back, needing some space and distance between her and Zane. She couldn't think straight when he was standing so close. She couldn't risk letting her emotions get the better of her. She might say or do something to jeopardize what they already had, which was a good friendship. A very good friendship…

Gabrielle Meyer lives in central Minnesota on the banks of the Mississippi River with her husband and four young children. As an employee of the Minnesota Historical Society, she fell in love with the rich history of her state and enjoys writing fictional stories inspired by real people and events. Gabrielle can be found at www.gabriellemeyer.com, where she writes about her passion for history, Minnesota and her faith.

Books by Gabrielle Meyer

Love Inspired

A Mother's Secret
Unexpected Christmas Joy
A Home for Her Baby
Snowed in for Christmas

Love Inspired Historical

A Mother in the Making
A Family Arrangement
Inherited: Unexpected Family
The Gift of Twins

Visit the Author Profile page
at Harlequin.com for more titles.

Snowed in for Christmas

Gabrielle Meyer

LOVE INSPIRED
INSPIRATIONAL ROMANCE

LOVE INSPIRED®

INSPIRATIONAL ROMANCE

Recycling programs
for this product may
not exist in your area.

ISBN-13: 978-1-335-56734-5

Snowed in for Christmas

Love Inspired
22 Adelaide St. West, 40th Floor
Toronto, Ontario M5H 4E3, Canada
www.Harlequin.com

Printed in U.S.A.

Though your sins be as scarlet, they shall be as white as snow; though they be red like crimson, they shall be as wool.
—*Isaiah* 1:18

To my son, Judah.
Your smile, your perpetual joy and
your easygoing nature bring so much happiness
to the world. I love you to the moon and back.

Chapter One

❧

Snowflakes danced against the large windows of Lakepoint Lodge as Olivia Butler readjusted the historic picture of the resort hanging near the front door. It was a good reminder to her, and to all the guests who would eventually stay at the resort, that the place had undergone a complete renovation. It was even more impressive than it had been in 1947, the year the main lodge had been built.

But Liv wasn't really thinking about what year the lodge was built, or even how much work she and her family had poured into the place over the past twelve months. All she could think about was greeting the travel journalist who was about to arrive to spend the holidays with her and her family as he worked on a feature article for *Minnesota Moments Magazine*.

The article would not only highlight her parents' resort, but it could also be the jump start Liv's interior design firm needed to take it to the next level. She had been working hard in the Timber Falls area for the past six years but would love to expand to other parts of Minnesota. The central lakes country was probably the most lucrative market outside of the Minneapolis/Saint Paul metro area, with so many Twin Cities residents owning lake homes.

A black SUV appeared in the parking lot at the base of Lakepoint Lodge and Liv breathed a sigh of relief. Snow had been falling for over an hour and she hadn't been sure the journalist would get past the county roads leading to the resort. The forecast had changed in the last twenty minutes and their area was now in a winter storm warning. Hopefully Liv's parents were already on the road, heading toward the resort, or they might not make it tonight. They'd gone to Minneapolis to pick up the last load of furniture Liv had designed, and they had hoped to get back in time to greet the journalist themselves. After all, it was their resort—a sort of semiretirement they had purchased last year when her dad left his job with the City of Marshall.

The journalist got out of his SUV with

a couple of children climbing out from the back. He stood for a second, looking up at the lodge and then slowly turned to take in the whole resort. She was too far away to see his face or his reaction, but she imagined he was thinking the same thing she had thought the first time she saw the property. It was like being transported back in time to the late 1940s.

The main lodge dominated the property, sitting on a point in Lake Madeline, one of the largest and most magnificent lakes in Minnesota. There were dozens of smaller log cabins along the shoreline and other buildings that served the guests during the summer months. A boathouse, a bait shop, a candy shop and more were now blanketed with a thick covering of snow. The lake was frozen over and icehouses were spread out on the massive sheet of ice in no particular order.

Whether or not her parents made it back tonight, Liv was in charge of greeting the journalist and his family. He'd called his editor, who had called Dad and Mom, to see if he could bring along his family for the holiday stay. He'd be at the resort through New Year's. Fourteen whole days to see what the resort had to offer. Liv had cautiously agreed to be there, as well, knowing it wouldn't be easy to spend that much time with her parents.

She crossed her arms as she watched the journalist's children run in the snowy parking lot. They twirled and danced, picking up handfuls of snow to toss in the air. From where she stood, she could tell they were little girls. One wore a purple coat, the other a pink coat.

Thankfully, Liv's two older brothers would be coming with their wives and children in a few days. They'd be a good buffer for Liv and her parents who struggled to see eye-to-eye. Liv's nieces and nephews would also make great playmates for the journalist's kids.

But, despite the excitement of seeing her nieces and nephews again, a pang filled Liv's heart as it usually did when her family gathered. They never brought up her pain, nor had she ever spoken of it to anyone—not even her best friend and business partner, Piper Evans. No one outside her immediate family knew Liv had become a mom at the age of seventeen or that she had only seen her baby girl for a few minutes before she was taken away to be adopted. Every time the family gathered, there was always an empty chair, at least in Liv's heart and mind. A spot that should have been filled by her own daughter, who would be eleven by now.

Liv took a deep, cleansing breath, and pushed aside the memories. She needed to focus on the journalist and his family right now. After they came inside, she'd show them to their suite and then see if they wanted something to eat. Her mother had made sure the kitchen was overstocked for the holidays, so they would have no fear of starvation. Then, if they weren't too tired, she thought she might take them sledding. There was a whole list of things she had planned for the family to enjoy during their stay.

The journalist went to the back of his SUV as the girls continued to play in the snow. Liv put on her thick fur-lined coat and slipped on her boots. No doubt they could use some help with their luggage, and she was the only one there to offer assistance. With all the renovations, the resort wasn't technically open for visitors, yet, so they had no staff on hand. They would have a soft opening after the New Year to iron out the kinks and then gear up for their big grand opening on Memorial Day weekend when the heavier summer traffic would start. The main focus of the article in *Minnesota Moments Magazine* would be about the history of the resort, as well as the renovations. Everyone had agreed that giving the journalist full access to the resort, before visitors were present, would help him focus on the elements he was most interested in covering.

Liv pushed open the heavy door and stepped onto the wide front deck. There was space out there for several tables and chairs, giving people a magnificent view of the lake. For now, all but a dozen tables and chairs were pushed under the eaves, covered in tarps for the winter. Her father had set up a gas fire table near the door in case the family wanted to enjoy an outdoor gathering over the holidays.

The deck and steps were covered in snow, though Liv had just cleared them thirty minutes ago. The snow was falling fast and thick from the dark clouds overhead. It gathered on her hair and shoulders, and little cold pricks landed on her face before melting.

She couldn't help but smile at the enthusiasm of the little girls or ignore the fact that the journalist had brought the children alone. That was odd. Her parents had assumed he was bringing his whole family. Liv didn't know much at all about this writer, except that he was a travel journalist who was new to *Minnesota Moments Magazine*. She didn't even know his name. The editor who sent him was a friend of her parents and Liv's dad and mom had made all the arrangements.

The girls stopped twirling and smiled up at Liv while their dad was still at the back of the SUV, out of sight. They were beautiful little girls with no hint of shyness. The younger one had big brown eyes, while the older one studied Liv with marble-blue eyes. They were bundled up in thick coats, stocking caps and mittens, but their winter gear could not hide their happiness or enthusiasm.

"Hello," the older girl said, a pretty smile showing off two perfect dimples. She extended her hand in a very grown-up gesture, though she looked to be about ten. "I'm Miley, what's your name?"

Liv smiled and shook her hand. "It's nice to meet you, Miley. I'm Liv. Welcome to Lakepoint Lodge."

"That's my sister, Alexis." Miley pointed to the younger girl who looked to be about five.

"Hello, Alexis," Liv said. "It's nice to meet you."

Alexis just giggled and ran toward the back of the SUV where her father was getting out their suitcases. He must have heard the exchange because he moved away from the vehicle and came around the corner, a smile on his handsome face.

But he stopped at the sight of Liv, his smile falling.

Liv's heartbeat slowed for a second as a hint of recognition tugged at her brain, but then it sped up again, beating harder as she realized who he was. Her legs weakened and she began to tremble all over.

"Liv." Zane Harris stared at her, his face filled with shock and dismay. "What are you doing here?"

It had been eleven years since she'd seen him and she'd never once tried to find him. She hadn't searched for him online, hadn't inquired about him to any of their old friends—nothing. For the past eleven years, she'd wanted to forget he'd ever been a part of her life.

Now here he stood, looking older and much more handsome than he'd been as an eighteen-year-old boy.

"Hello, Zane," she finally responded. Her voice sounded hoarse and pathetic, even to her own ears.

They stood there for a long time, neither one speaking as the snow continued to fall all around them. Zane wore a black wool coat with a black stocking cap and black-rimmed glasses. His shoulders were broader, his face more defined and he'd even grown a bit taller.

A day-old beard gave him a rugged appearance, especially with the snow as a background.

He looked amazing.

"You look good, Liv," he finally said. "It's nice to see you."

Was it? She'd never thought she'd see him again.

His daughters stood near him, staring at Liv, curiosity in their eyes.

"Is this your place?" he asked, looking beyond her toward the lodge. "I didn't get any of the details from my editor before I came." He laughed, his tone revealing his discomfort. "I actually have never met my editor. I'm doing a freelance piece, hoping to land a permanent position on staff. They just told me where to be and when to get here."

"Daddy promised we could find a school and a house with a yard," Miley said. "We don't want to move anymore."

Liv's mind whirled as she continued to stare at Zane's family.

"That's nice," she finally said to the girl. "Don't you have a house?"

"We've been living in apartments all over the world," Miley said. "London, Dublin, Berlin, Paris, Rome." She ticked off the names of the cities on her fingers and shrugged.

"I'm a travel journalist," Zane explained, "so we've been privileged to live in some pretty amazing places." He put his hand on Miley's shoulder. "But now we're going to settle down and put in some roots, aren't we, Miley?"

The girl grinned up at her dad.

Zane Harris was the travel journalist she'd have to spend the next two weeks entertaining? Her pulse picked up speed. How on earth would she spend fourteen days with him, without dredging up the horrible past?

"So," he asked again, "is this your place?"

She shook her head, needing to take command of the situation. "This is my parents' resort. I—I was the interior designer and decorator, so they asked me to be here to show you around."

Zane pressed his lips together and nodded, though he didn't look pleased at the mention of her mom and dad. "How are your parents?"

Liv's mom and dad had not been kind to Zane eleven years ago. They'd laid all the blame of her pregnancy on him, though Liv knew she and Zane were both responsible. No doubt he remembered how badly they'd treated him.

"They're good." She paused, hoping to change the subject. "Would you like to get out of the cold?" She smiled at the girls, not wanting any of them to feel uncomfortable because of her. "I have some hot chocolate warming for you."

"Yes!" Both girls looked up at their dad for approval and he nodded. They ran toward the lodge without a second invitation.

Zane didn't move and once the girls were out of hearing range he said, "I'm sorry, Liv. I didn't know this was your parents' place. If I had, I would have asked for a different assignment."

She put on a smile, even if she didn't quite feel like smiling. The past was in the past. They'd both survived and had hopefully moved on. They were adults. They could handle a few days in each other's company.

"It's okay. I didn't know it would be you, either." She indicated his suitcases. "Would you like me to help?"

"Are you certain this is a good idea?" He glanced up toward the lodge and his girls.

Liv needed the magazine article written for the sake of her business and her parents' resort. She nodded. "It will be fine."

Zane didn't look convinced.

The snow began to fall faster and the wind had picked up. Zane stared at Liv Butler, never having expected to see her again. She was beautiful, even prettier than she'd been in high school. Her blue eyes were so vibrant it was hard to look at her. She carried herself with the grace and elegance of a dancer, and even though she was in a thick coat and boots, he could tell she had a great sense of style.

She always had.

He felt like an idiot just standing there, staring, but he couldn't help it. Though he'd traveled the world, met some amazing people and survived the death of his wife, being in Liv's presence made him feel like he was an untried eighteen-year-old boy again. He hadn't felt this uncertain or self-conscious since he was a teenager.

"Do you need help with your bags?" Liv asked again.

"No." He shook his head quickly. "We only have a few things. I've got it."

He went to the back of his SUV, happy to keep his hands and mind occupied.

Liv waited for him.

The girls had gone ahead and were standing on the deck of the lodge, throwing snow at one another. It did his heart good to see them laughing and playing. Since his wife had died two years ago, he'd tried to be both a dad and mom to them, but with their constant moving, his work and the need to homeschool them, he'd had little time to just be a dad. Bringing them back to Minnesota was going to change everything for them. He just needed to make sure he could get a permanent job so they wouldn't have to leave again. That's where the article came into play. If the editor liked his work, he promised Zane a full-time gig. They could finally settle into a house and find a school. He looked forward to taking a deep breath again.

"Your girls are beautiful," Liv said.

Zane looked at her sharply. Had Liv suspected that Miley was her daughter? If she had, she didn't show any signs of recognition. What would she say or do when she learned the truth?

The day Miley was born, Liv had only seen her for a moment and then the nurses had brought her to Zane in another room. He'd held her, his heart breaking, knowing he was losing Liv and Miley all at the same time. Zane's cousin and his wife were at the hospital, ready to take the baby home with them to Wisconsin. They had struggled with infertility for years and were going to adopt her. The plans were all in place. Within twenty-four hours, Liv had signed away her rights and her parents had whisked her away, warning

Zane to never seek her out again. She was leaving their small Southern Minnesota town and going to live with a relative somewhere. He never asked where.

The week Miley was born was a blur. Zane had an appointment to meet with social services to sign away his parental rights, but the hour before his appointment, his cousin had called Zane's mom and told her the adoption had been stopped. His cousin's wife had changed her mind after just a few days at home. They didn't want her anymore.

No one saw it coming, least of all Zane.

The baby was brought to Zane and his parents, and they had a long, hard talk about what it would take for Zane to raise her. He'd been scared, but he wanted to keep her. Couldn't imagine sending her to someone he didn't know.

So, with his parents' financial help, he had moved to Chicago to attend college and then worked hard to get his dream job as a travel journalist. Nothing had been easy, but he'd made it work. He'd also met Tanya, his wife, his freshman year in college. She'd loved Miley from the start, and they'd been inseparable. By the time he and Tanya married the summer they graduated, Miley had called her mom. They'd never had a reason to tell her any differently.

And so, Miley never knew that Tanya wasn't her biological mother, or that she and Alexis were only half sisters. Zane never intended to keep it from Miley, but there had not been a good time to tell her. After Tanya died in the car accident in Rome two years ago, all thoughts of telling Miley had fled completely.

"They seem really excited to be here," Liv said, smiling at the girls.

Zane had to pull his mind out of the past. How long until Liv learned the truth? Eventually she'd figure it out, wouldn't she? He didn't want to keep it from her, but things were happening so fast, he wasn't prepared for this moment. He needed time to think.

"They've heard me telling them all about Minnesota Christmases for most of their lives." He smiled. "It took me a while, but I finally made it back here."

"What about their mom?" she asked quietly, almost tentative. "Will she be joining you?"

Zane trudged through the snow with Liv, his arms laden with suitcases. "She died. Two years ago. A cab accident while we were living in Rome. Both she and the driver were killed." And the man who had been with Tanya at the time, though Zane tried never to think of him nor mention him. What was the point? It just reminded him of his own guilt.

"I'm so sorry." Liv stopped, her eyes filled with sorrow for him. "How horrible."

He swallowed the grief, like he'd been doing for the past two years, and continued toward the lodge. "It's been a tough couple of years, but the girls and I are doing a lot better now."

Time had a way of softening the pain, though it never faded completely. He could talk about Tanya now without his gut wrenching. The girls talked about her all the time.

"I thought about bringing the girls back to the States at that time," he continued. "My parents are now living in Phoenix and they told me I could go there, but Arizona isn't my home. I thought it better to keep living the way we had been for a while. I didn't want to tear them away from everything they knew and loved all at once, and when we were ready, I wanted to bring them to Minnesota and raise them here."

"Do you think you'll go back to Marshall?"

Zane shook his head. Ironically, he hadn't planned to ever return to their hometown, afraid he might run into Liv or her family, knowing they didn't want anything to do with him or Miley. They'd assumed the adoption had happened and he thought it would be easier to let them continue thinking that. "There's nothing there for me. I was actually thinking about settling down somewhere in the central lakes area. I've always loved it here. I just hope the girls enjoy it as much as I do."

"I'm happy we can offer them a nice Christmas. My brothers and their kids will be here in a few days, and your girls will have children their age to play with."

"Good. They haven't had anyone but each other for the most part." Zane stopped and Liv stopped, too. "I just can't get over how amazing it is that we've run into each other here, so far from Marshall." Their hometown was over two hundred miles southwest of Lakepoint Lodge. "What are the odds?"

Liv shrugged. "When my parents decided to buy a resort, this one was for sale."

"That's incredible." But maybe it wasn't so strange. Maybe it was God's way of orchestrating a reunion for Liv and Miley, though neither one knew it yet. And how strange that Miley would get to meet her cousins, too? He was still having a hard time believing he and

Liv found each other again—especially when neither one had been looking for the other.

Zane just hoped and prayed it would go well, because he knew, without a doubt, that before he left Lakepoint Lodge, he would have to tell Liv Butler the truth.

The daughter she hadn't seen in eleven years was standing only a few feet away from her.

Chapter Two

Liv pushed open the heavy front doors of the lodge. They were made of ancient pine logs and were scarred with the passage of time and use. How many people had entered through these doors over the years, seeking refuge and rest on the shores of Lake Madeline?

"We've reserved the best suite in the lodge for your family." Liv held the door open for Zane and his girls to pass through. Her heart broke for them, knowing this was only the second Christmas without their mom. Though she struggled with her parents, Liv couldn't imagine losing one of them, especially so young.

"It's really starting to come down out there." Zane set their luggage on the rug and shook the snow off his shoulders and arms.

"I hope my parents are okay." Liv was certain her dad would stop and stay in a hotel if it got really bad. He was cautious to a fault.

But if they did stop at a hotel, that would leave Liv alone with Zane and his daughters—a prospect she wasn't ready to think about just yet.

The main room of the lodge had high ceilings with thick beams, a massive rock fireplace, pine-plank floors and board-and-batten walls, also made of pine and darkened over time. Oversize furniture flanked the fireplace and a registration desk stretched across the back of the room. A fire crackled in the hearth.

Miley and Alexis looked up at the tall ceilings, their eyes wide.

"It's beautiful," Zane said, "and exactly how I pictured a Minnesota Northwoods lodge." He glanced at Liv. "And you did the decorating?"

She was suddenly reminded why he came. He would write an article about the lodge, including her work. Her heart raced and she felt nervous again. "Yes. I did all the redecorating and did the interior design work for the renovated spaces. Most of the suites in the lodge were completely redesigned, but the log cabins along the lake just needed a bit of a facelift. The lobby and dining hall didn't need much help, but the owner's apartment was completely redone." She waved her hand, as if to push it all aside. "There'll be time for all of that later. How about I show you to your suite so the girls can get out of those warm clothes and we can rustle up some hot chocolate and snacks?"

The girls nodded their eager agreement and Liv walked toward the left, where a large set of stairs dominated the corner of the lobby. They went up to the guest suites, and down to the kitchen and dining hall, which also served as a ballroom.

"We've put you in the presidential suite, overlooking the bay," Liv told Zane. "There are two bedrooms, two bathrooms and a large sitting room and kitchenette for you to enjoy while you're here—though my mom has a full menu planned and you won't need to cook a thing."

"This is amazing," Zane said. "We've been guests at places all over the world, but nothing has been as homey or charming as Lakepoint Lodge. Your parents have a gold mine here."

"When they first purchased the property, it had been run-down for years." They'd put a lot of time, money and sweat into the resort, and Liv hoped and prayed their sacrifices would pay off. "My brothers and their families have all invested and plan to work here over the summer."

"And what about you?" Zane asked.

"I hope to expand my interior design firm."

"Do you live nearby?"

"About fifty miles south of here, in Timber Falls."

"Home of Esther Lund, the movie star," Zane said with a smile on his face. "And the largest arts-and-crafts fair in the Upper Midwest."

"That's the place." She couldn't help but smile, as well, since those were the two things Timber Falls was most known for.

She'd gone to Timber Falls to live with her aunt and uncle after giving birth to her daughter and had spent her senior year of high school there. After she went to college, she returned to take care of her ailing aunt and had started her design firm, as well as a weddings-and-events company with her friend Piper. The town wasn't big enough for either business to be full-time, but if the magazine article was a success, perhaps her design business would finally grow and expand outside Timber Falls.

Liv unlocked the door to the presidential

suite. She pushed it open, and bright light filled the darkened hallway.

"Whoa," Miley said as she rushed into the room and went to the glass doors facing the frozen lake. A balcony lay just beyond the doors and would be a beautiful place to sit on a starry summer evening. On either side of the sitting room were doors, leading to their bedrooms. A thick rug covered the wood floors, and a large fireplace filled one wall.

"This is perfect, Liv," Zane said. "Thank you."

"Our pleasure."

Miley and Alexis immediately began to peel off their layers of outdoor clothing. For the first time, Liv saw that Miley had a head of blond curls and Alexis had dark brown. They looked as opposite as two sisters could look, but they were both so sweet.

It was Alexis who caught her attention. The little girl had the most bizarre outfit that Liv had ever seen. She wore a pair of red-and-white-striped tights, a bright pink tutu and a neon orange shirt with a pumpkin in the center. Her hair was disheveled, but there were lime-green barrettes askew at the top of her head.

Zane laid his coat on the back of a chair,

a grin on his face. "She picks out her own outfits."

"She has a unique eye for fashion."

Alexis giggled and did a little twirl.

"When you're ready, you can come down to the dining hall." Liv started to move toward the door. "It's on the lowest level—" She paused, midsentence.

Miley had slipped her hair behind her right ear, revealing a familiar birthmark—one that matched Liv's exactly.

But why would Zane's daughter have Liv's—

The room began to spin as Liv's breathing became shallow. She had to reach out to put her hand on the back of a chair, or she was afraid she'd faint.

Was Miley her daughter?

Miley glanced at Liv, and for the first time, Liv recognized the marble-blue eyes. They were exactly like Liv's. So was her nose and mouth. With her blond hair curled around her face, she looked just like Liv had at that age. How could she not have known immediately? How had she just spent the past ten minutes with her own daughter and not known?

Zane looked from Miley to Liv, uncertainty in his gaze.

She stared at him for what felt like an eternity, and then she glanced at Miley again. The little girl took off her boots and set them by the fireplace, completely unaware that Liv's world had just turned on its side.

"Liv." Zane came toward her, but she backed up.

What was happening? Why did he have their daughter? She was supposed to be adopted by his cousin. That had been the plan. So then why did she call him Dad, and why was she with him?

Liv couldn't catch her breath.

"We need to talk," he said quietly to her. "Can we step into the hall?"

Liv wasn't even sure if she could walk to the hall unassisted, let alone try to form coherent words.

"I need to talk to Miss Butler for a minute, girls," Zane said to his daughters. "Choose which room you'd like to share and get your things settled. I'll be right back."

The girls did as he said, eagerly running to one of the rooms as Zane took Liv's hand and led her out of the suite.

She felt like she was sleepwalking as he opened the door and drew her out into the hall.

He closed the door gently and turned to her,

his brown eyes searching her face. "I know you must have a thousand questions."

She would, if she could get her brain to start working properly again. "Is she…?"

He nodded. "She's your daughter."

Shock soon turned to confusion. "How?" she asked, shaking her head. "I don't understand. Have you had her this whole time?"

He nodded again.

"But you signed away your rights, just like I did." The hall was dark, even with the soft glow of the wall sconces. "She should be with your cousin and his wife." That's how she'd always imagined their daughter growing up. In a house with his cousin and wife, somewhere in Wisconsin. Wasn't that where they lived?

"It didn't go through. They chose to stop the adoption before I signed any papers." He put his hands in his coat pockets. "It wasn't the plan, but everything happened so quickly. My parents agreed to help me."

"But…" She opened her mouth to protest. He wasn't supposed to keep her. They were both going to move on with their lives, as if nothing had happened. Wasn't that what their parents had agreed to? It's what she had tried to do. "Why didn't you tell me?"

He leaned against the wall and took his

cap off. He gripped it in his hands, his dark brown hair curling in disarray. "I never meant to hurt you or anyone else." His eyes pleaded with her to understand. "Your parents made it very clear that I should not reach out to you again. They wanted you to go on with your life. I didn't think you'd want to know. And to be honest, I thought you wouldn't care."

"Not care?" Her voice caught as eleven years of pain and sorrow threatened to choke her. Her life had been a nightmare since the day she'd given her baby away. She'd suffered awful dreams, panic attacks and horrible self-hatred. How could she have given up her own baby without a fight? The only explanation was that she was heartless, and it was proven to her each time a relationship failed. She had never cried once—not over the loss of anyone who walked out on her.

How could she cry about someone leaving her when she had walked out on her own daughter? She didn't have the right.

"The last time I saw you—" Zane crossed his arms as he watched her, his eyes full of pain "—you didn't even want to hold the baby." He lifted a shoulder. "You were like stone. I really didn't think you cared."

Stone.

She remembered that day like it was yesterday and closed her eyes, wishing she could push away the pain. She had wanted to hold her daughter, but her mother had forbidden her. Told her it would be too painful and Liv had believed her. "How else was I supposed to cope?" she whispered, opening her eyes again. She'd never spoken to anyone about that day. To do so now felt almost wrong. But Zane had been there. He knew what it had been like, yet he hadn't said goodbye to their daughter like she had. "I was seventeen," she said, her voice filled with more anger than hurt now. "I didn't have a choice. Unlike your parents, mine wanted to pretend it had never happened."

His face was shadowed by the light. "I'm sorry, Liv."

She shook her head, a half cry, half laugh falling off her lips. "I have no one to blame but myself. At least you did the honorable thing. You could have found someone else to adopt her, but you sacrificed your life to raise her."

And what had Liv done? She'd gone on, pretending nothing was different. She'd served herself and no one else.

"Neither one of us avoided sacrifice." His eyes were so understanding—so forgiving—

Liv was afraid she'd start to weep. And if she started, how would she ever stop?

"Does she know?" Liv whispered.

Zane didn't speak for a long time as he studied her, and then he finally shook his head no. "I met my wife when Miley was less than a year old." He shrugged. "She has never known anything different. Tanya and I planned to tell her when she was a little older, but then Tanya—" He paused, as if he couldn't bring himself to talk about her death. "I haven't thought much about it since."

Liv wrapped her arms around her waist, the pain mounting. If there had even been a glimmer of hope that Miley might ever know her as her biological mother, it was now snuffed out. She could never tell her that the mother she had known and loved, and who was now dead, was not her biological mom. It would be cruel.

"If you want us to leave," Zane said, "we should go now, before the girls get settled."

Liv shook her head. She couldn't make those precious children leave now, not when they were so excited to be here. And, even if she couldn't tell Miley who she was, she wanted desperately to get to know her. She had never thought she'd have the privilege, yet the rare gift had been offered. She couldn't turn it aside now. "I don't want you to leave."

"What about your parents?"

Liv briefly closed her eyes again. How would she explain all this to her parents? How would they treat Zane? "I'll talk to them." Her parents understood the importance of an article in the magazine, even more than Liv did. They needed the free publicity if they wanted their resort to succeed. "We'll make it work."

"Are you sure?" He studied her again. "They made it clear they didn't want me to contact you ever again."

"You didn't purposely find me. And, I'm an adult now, Zane. It's not up to them anymore."

He nodded, his dark eyes so kind.

A well of affection for him bubbled up, out of nowhere. She had been the one to walk away. She hadn't put up a fight for him or for Miley. Yet, he was showing her incredible grace and mercy.

She'd almost forgotten how much she had loved him eleven years ago.

But even if they hadn't gotten pregnant, or been forced to go their separate ways, she was certain it would have ended, just like all her other failed relationships. She didn't have the capability to love—not like other people did. He would have eventually learned the truth and would have left, just like the others.

"I want you to stay," she said. "You and your girls deserve a nice holiday."

He was quiet for a moment before nodding. "I promised them a happy Christmas and told them we could stay in one place for a little while. I'd hate to disappoint them."

"Then we won't." Liv took a deep breath and straightened her shoulders. "And you don't have to worry. I won't say anything to Miley." Her voice caught, and she had to take a second to compose herself again. "I would never knowingly hurt that little girl more than I already have."

Zane pushed away from the wall and set his hand on Liv's arm. "You haven't hurt her, Liv. You gave her the greatest gift in the world. Life."

She nibbled on her bottom lip, wishing she could believe him. But in her heart she knew that abandonment overshadowed any gift she might have given her daughter.

Twenty minutes later, Zane held Alexis's and Miley's hands as they walked down the wide staircase into the massive dining hall. It was on the lowest level of the lodge, which was built into the side of a hill, offering a bank of windows to look out at the lake, as well as wide doors opening onto a snow-covered patio. The dining hall had the same Northwoods flavor as the lobby and boasted a rock fireplace, much like the one upstairs, as well as pine-plank floors, scratched and dented over the course of time.

The girls were eager for the promised hot chocolate, but Zane wasn't quite as excited. The hardest thing he'd ever done in his life was face Liv in that hallway. He hadn't had time to think about what he should say or how she might react. He'd always assumed she was cold and indifferent to their daughter, but her reaction told him a different story. Liv had suffered far more than he had ever imagined. There had been so much pain and regret in her eyes, he hurt for her.

He dreaded facing her again, and the thought of fourteen more days in her company seemed daunting. Not because he disliked her—on the contrary, he'd always thought Liv Butler was the coolest girl he'd ever known—but because none of this could be easy for her and he didn't quite know how to proceed. They were all walking uncharted territory. The least he could do was make the path smoother for Liv.

"Wow!" Miley said as she let go of Zane's

hand and ran to stand under a buffalo head mounted to the fireplace. "I've never seen one up close before."

Alexis also dropped her father's hand and joined her sister, her eyes huge.

"I see you've found Billy." Liv entered the room with a tray of mugs and a steaming pot.

"Billy?" Miley asked.

"Billy the Buffalo." She set the tray down on a table and walked up to the girls, uncertainty in her movements. "He's been here since the lodge was built, over seventy years ago, but he's even older than that."

"Where'd he come from?" Alexis asked, her thumb slipping into her mouth in a habit Zane had tried to break. He reached over and pulled it out.

"From the prairies of North Dakota," Liv said. "He's over a hundred years old. The man who built this lodge had him placed there, and he's been overseeing all the meals and dances in this room ever since."

"There are dances in here?" Miley's blue eyes grew round. She had studied ballet wherever they had lived. It was one of her favorite things in the world and something that stayed consistent, no matter where they moved.

"Probably not the kind of dances you're thinking about," Zane told her. He glanced at

Liv, who had taken off her coat and was wearing a long-sleeve dark blue shirt tucked into jeans and a thick knitted scarf. The color of her shirt made her blue eyes sparkle. "Miley is a ballet dancer."

Liv's eyes lit up. "Ballet?"

Miley grinned and did a pirouette. "I *live* to dance," she said in a very theatrical voice.

Zane and Liv laughed and Liv shook her head. "I took ballet lessons almost all my life. I still take an adult class now."

"You do?" Miley was clearly impressed.

Liv nodded.

Zane knew Liv had been a dancer. He'd watched her on stage many times. He also knew it would be something she could share with Miley.

"You and Miley have a lot in common," Zane said, his voice lowered a bit. "You might be surprised."

Liv glanced at him, her lips trembling a bit as she smiled.

"Do you still have dances here?" Miley asked.

"My parents have talked about having a dance this summer, when the resort is full of families." Liv went to the mugs and poured the hot chocolate. Steam curled up from the warm liquid.

"Can we come, Daddy?" Miley asked.

"Maybe." Zane smiled at his daughter. "It would be fun to come back this summer, wouldn't it?"

"We could swim in the lake," Alexis added.

"I wish we could swim now." Miley walked to Liv's side and inspected the hot chocolate. If he knew his daughter, she was probably trying to figure out which one was the fullest.

"The winter is fun, too," Liv informed them. "I have plans to take you sledding, ice skating, ice fishing, cross-country skiing and more." She handed Miley a cup of hot chocolate and then handed the next to Alexis. "The snow also gives us a great excuse to curl up by the fireside and play board games." Finally, she handed a cup to Zane. Their fingers brushed and she glanced up at him.

She was prettier than ever. Her blue eyes were so captivating, he had a hard time looking away. They were so similar to Miley's, it was startling.

"And," Liv continued, "we have a surprise for everyone on Christmas Day." She grinned at Miley and then at Alexis. "Do you like horses?"

Both girls nodded eagerly.

"The surprise involves horses, but that's all I'm going to tell you."

Alexis looked up at Zane, excitement in her grin. She especially loved horses.

A timer went off in the kitchen.

"The cookies are ready," Liv said.

"Cookies?" Miley's mouth fell open. "Did you make cookies, too?"

"My mom made the dough before she left this morning. I just put a few in the oven before you came down. Would you like to help me get them out? If your dad says it's okay," she added quickly, glancing at Zane.

"I think that would be a great idea." Zane nodded at Liv. He wanted her to get to know their daughter. He hoped she wanted it, too.

The pair walked toward the kitchen together, Miley at Liv's side, talking incessantly as Miley tended to do.

Zane and Alexis took a seat at the table and a couple minutes later, Liv and Miley returned with a plate full of warm chocolate-chip cookies. The girls talked excitedly about sledding and ice skating while Liv and Zane just sat and listened. Liv answered all their questions, but her gaze rested on Miley several times.

He wished he knew what she was thinking. Her life had just changed irrevocably in the past hour. What did she want to know? What did she want to say?

When the girls were full of hot chocolate and cookies, they asked to be excused and left the table to explore the rest of the large dining hall. There were black-and-white pictures of the resort hanging on the walls, other mounted animals and a corner with games and toys for children to amuse themselves while their parents visited.

Zane and Liv sat at the table, their hot chocolate growing cold.

"I want you to feel comfortable with Miley," Zane told her, his voice low enough that the girls couldn't hear him from where they played. "She's an amazing child. You'll love her."

Liv looked down at her hot chocolate and nodded. "I can tell she's amazing. You've done a great job raising her. She's smart, kind and very polite."

"Don't let her fool you." Zane laughed. "She's also stubborn, headstrong and assertive when she wants to get her way."

Liv laughed gently and twisted her mug on the table. "She's perfect. Both of the girls are. Alexis looks a lot like you with her dark hair and eyes. Miley looks…"

"Just like you."

Liv finally glanced up at Zane, and he

could tell by the look in her eyes that she agreed.

Zane pushed aside his hot chocolate and put his elbows up on the table, clasping his hands. "I know this is all happening really fast, Liv. I wish both you and I had been given time to prepare ourselves, but I trust that God knows what He's doing. I had always planned to tell Miley about you—I just didn't know when." He shrugged. "I don't think there will ever be a better time than now."

Her eyes grew wide and full of panic. "Now?"

"Well, not *right* now. But definitely before we leave the resort." He paused. "Unless—" He didn't even want to consider that she would refuse to tell Miley the truth. It didn't seem fair to their daughter, yet it was Liv's choice. She'd walked away eleven years ago without a fight. It wasn't Zane's place to force her back into Miley's life. "Unless you don't want her to know."

Liv glanced in Miley's direction. "More than anything, I want her to know." Her eyes filled with tears, which she blinked away. "But she already has a mom. Wouldn't it be cruel to tell her about me now? What if she doesn't want to know me?"

"It would be even worse if I didn't tell her.

She deserves to know and the sooner the better." Guilt weighed heavy on his heart. "I should have told her a long time ago—from the beginning."

Liv was quiet for a moment, and then she said, "What happens after we tell her? Do I just disappear again?"

Zane's pulse beat a little faster as he studied Liv. "What do you want to happen?"

The space between them became still as Liv stared at him, hope and uncertainty mingling in her gaze. "Do I have a choice?"

"You've always had a choice, Liv."

She shook her head. "Not when I was seventeen. My parents didn't give me any choices." She dropped her gaze. "But I didn't fight them for choices, either."

"What about now?" he asked. "What do you want?"

"If we tell her, do you think it would be okay to let Miley decide how much she wants me in her life?" She watched him closely. "Is that an option?"

His heart warmed as he smiled and nodded. "I think that's a great option."

She took a deep breath. "Then I'd like her to know. But not yet," she added quickly. "First, I want to spend time with her. I don't want her to find out I'm her biological mother when we're still strangers. It doesn't seem right."

"Okay." He nodded. "Whenever you're ready, just let me know."

An appreciative smile lifted her lips. "Thank you, Zane. I know you don't have to be this nice."

Though Zane had always thought Liv's treatment toward him and Miley had been cold and indifferent at the end, he'd never harbored any anger or resentment toward her. They were young and they'd both made mistakes—suffering the consequences in unique ways. If they were going to make the best of it, they'd have to work together. And that's exactly what he planned to do.

Chapter Three

While Zane took the girls back to their suite for Alexis to nap, Liv went to the room where she'd be staying over the holidays. It was a guest suite on the second floor, close to Zane's suite. She stood near one of the large windows overlooking Lake Madeline and pulled her cell phone out of her pocket. On the clearest days, she struggled to get good reception, but on a cloudy day like today, it was even worse. The snow continued to fall, and the wind blew even harder, creating near-whiteout conditions.

She had missed a call from her mom earlier.

It was already midafternoon and her parents should have been back at the resort by now.

Liv tapped her mom's name on her phone

and it immediately began to ring. Mom picked up a moment later.

"Hello, Olivia," she said. "I was hoping you'd have enough reception to call me back."

"Hi, Mom." Liv sat on the arm of the oversize sofa in her sitting room as she looked outside. "How are the roads?"

"Terrible. They closed Highway 94 right after we got off in Saint Cloud, and Highway 10 is even worse. We stopped to spend the night. I hope you don't mind entertaining our guests on your own."

Did she? At first, the thought of being alone with Zane and his children was overwhelming, but now that she knew Miley was her daughter, a part of her wanted her parents to stay away as long as possible. They'd only complicate matters more. "It's okay."

"Who is he? Is he nice? What about his wife and kids? Are they nice?" Mom was the queen of questions. More often than not, she didn't even wait for, or want, the answers. "Is he old or young? Does he like the resort? Oh, I wish we could have been there to see his reaction. We've done so much work, it's rewarding to see someone else appreciate it. He does appreciate the work, doesn't he?"

"He's impressed," Liv said. "But—" She paused, uncertain how to tell her mom.

"You'll be really surprised to find out who he is."

"Why? Who is he? Someone famous?"

Liv swallowed and then stood, pressing her forehead against the cold glass. "Zane Harris."

There was a pause on the other end, and then her mom inhaled a sharp breath. "Zane Harris? *The* Zane Harris? The—the—"

Father of my child? Liv wanted to finish the sentence for her. "Yes, Mom. It's Zane."

"But, h-how?" she stuttered. "Why didn't I know it was Zane?"

"I don't know. Didn't you ask your editor friend who he was sending?"

"It didn't occur to me to ask." Mom's voice had taken on a frantic pitch. "What will we do?"

"What can we do? He's a well-respected journalist. I just looked him up online, and he's done freelance work for dozens of domestic and international travel magazines. He also has a very popular blog, and he gets paid to endorse resorts and destinations around the world. We'd be foolish to send him away."

"Bob," Mom said to Liv's dad, who must have been in the room with her, "did you hear what your daughter just said?"

"I heard, Marilyn."

Liv must be on speaker phone.

"What should we do?" Mom asked Dad.

"I guess it should be up to Liv. What do you think, kiddo?"

"Why should it be up to Olivia?" Mom asked.

"Because of what *happened* to her."

Neither one said anything for a moment, and Liv knew they were communicating with their eyes, trying to read what the other was thinking without including her. They'd done it for as long as she could remember.

"I'm okay with Zane being here," Liv said, her heart pounding harder, knowing she needed to tell them the rest. "He brought his children with him."

"Children?" Mom's curious voice was close to the phone. "What about his wife?"

"She passed away two years ago." Liv crossed one arm over her chest and hugged herself.

"That's too bad." Mom sighed. "Isn't that too bad, Bob?"

"It's a tough break, that's for sure."

"He has two little girls." Liv wished she could have this conversation with her parents face-to-face, but she didn't want to wait until they arrived. "And the oldest is—" Liv choked on the words.

"The oldest is what?" Mom asked.

There was no way to get around the truth. "My daughter."

A long pause ensued and Liv closed her eyes, praying her parents wouldn't freak out.

"Oh, Liv," Dad finally said, his voice both sad and disappointed.

Liv sat on the sofa, her legs weak and shaking.

"How in the world?" Mom's voice was high-pitched. "Tell me, Olivia. How in the world?"

Liv told them how it had come about, trying desperately to keep her composure.

"I'm floored," Mom said. "Simply floored. What right does *that* man have to come to *our* resort, with *his* daughter, and expect us to open our arms? What right does he have, Bob?"

"He didn't know it was us," Liv defended him, her pulse picking up speed. "And she's my daughter, too."

"And, what?" Mom asked. "You're going to just pick up where you left off eleven years ago? Start playing house with him and his family?"

"What are you talking about?" Liv's anger and frustration mounted. "We're both reeling from this. Neither one of us saw it coming."

"Does the child know who you are?"

"Her name is Miley, and, no, she doesn't know."

"Well, at least there's that."

"Mom." Liv took a deep breath, trying to slow down her heart rate and keep control of the situation. "Zane and I are dealing with this situation. We plan to tell her when the time is right. But, for now, they'll stay through the holidays, just like they planned, and Zane will write the article for *Minnesota Moments Magazine*, just like he planned."

"What about after the holidays? What then, Olivia?"

"We will deal with it when the time comes."

"You need to have a plan. Being careless is what got you in this position to begin with, or don't you remember?"

Liv put her hand over her face. "Mom, I'm twenty-eight years old. You don't need to remind me."

"I don't like that tone, Liv," Dad warned. "Your mom is just concerned."

"I don't want to have to pick up the pieces again," Mom said.

"Like the last time," Liv asked, her voice sharp, "when you dropped me off at Aunt Betty's house the day after my daughter was born so you wouldn't have to deal with me?"

A dead silence hung in the air, and Liv immediately regretted her words. Their relationship had been grievously injured after her pregnancy, and it was only within the past year that they had started putting it back together again. Her parents had been just as shaken up as her when Liv had become pregnant. "I'm sorry, Mom. It's been a long day."

"I'm sorry, too, Olivia." Mom had been trying, Liv had to give her that. "You're right. You're an adult now and you can handle your own issues. I just don't want you to get hurt again."

"I know."

"If you're okay with them being at the resort," Dad said, "then we're okay with it, too. We'll make it work."

"Thank you."

"Though, I can't promise your brothers will be okay with it," Mom warned.

Liv sighed. "They'll have to be okay with it."

There was a pause again, and then Mom said, "I was planning to make eggplant Parmesan for supper tonight. All the ingredients are in the kitchen. Since we won't be able to get there, you'll have to make supper."

Eggplant Parmesan? Liv had no idea how to make it, nor did she think the girls would enjoy it. She wasn't a horrible cook, but she definitely wasn't as accomplished as her mom in the kitchen. She'd have to look through the cupboards and refrigerator and see if she could figure out something else to serve. "When do you think you'll be able to get here?"

"I've been watching the forecast," Dad said, "and it looks like we're in a winter weather advisory until tomorrow evening. By the time they get the roads clear, it could be midafternoon the day after. We're still eighty miles away, so we might be able to get there by evening."

"The day after tomorrow?" Liv asked.

"At the earliest. We won't leave until it's safe to travel again."

Two or three days without her parents' interference sounded ideal.

"Okay," she said. "Stay safe and keep me informed."

"We will," Dad said. "You let us know if you need any help. Give us a call if you can't find something."

"I will. Thanks, Dad."

"And, Olivia?" Mom asked.

"Yes?"

"Just be smart. That's all I'm asking."

Liv wanted to roll her eyes. Ever since her unplanned pregnancy at the age of seventeen,

Liv had done nothing to get herself into trouble again. "You don't need to worry, Mom."

"You know I will."

"Okay. I'll chat with you later. Bye."

"Goodbye," her parents said in unison.

Liv hung up the phone and lay down on the sofa. No doubt her brothers would know all about Zane before they got to the resort in a couple of days. Her mom was probably already dialing their numbers. That left her just forty-eight hours to prepare herself and Zane for their arrival.

They'd be just as hard on Zane as her mom and dad, maybe even worse.

"You don't mind if I leave you here for a while?" Zane asked Miley, who was curled up on one of the sofas in their sitting room, a blanket around her shoulders and a book in hand. "Alexis will probably sleep for another half an hour or so, and I'd like to see if Liv needs help with supper."

"I don't mind," Miley said with a big smile. She was eleven and old enough to babysit her little sister for a bit and loved the responsibility. She'd been asking Zane if she could babysit for the past year, but he wasn't quite ready for her to stay with her sister completely alone.

"I'll just be downstairs if you need anything."

"It's okay, Daddy." She waved him away. "I can handle it."

He could hardly believe she was getting so old, or so mature. It seemed like just yesterday he'd held her in his arms for the first time.

"Have fun with Liv." She giggled and smiled, covering her mouth with her book.

Zane raised his eyebrows at her but didn't ask her to elaborate as he stepped out of their suite.

The sun had already set, and it was only five o'clock. He'd almost forgotten how quickly it grew dark in December in Minnesota. Alexis didn't usually sleep so long, but they'd been traveling since yesterday, leaving their rented flat in London only twenty-four hours ago. They had flown to Amsterdam with a short layover before their connecting flight to Minneapolis. He'd rented the SUV at the Minneapolis airport and then driven the two and a half hours to Lakepoint Lodge. They'd slept on their flights, but it would take some time for them to adjust to the time change. He'd have to wake Alexis up in thirty minutes, but then she'd probably crash again after supper.

When he reached the dining hall, the scent

of marinara filled his nose and he inhaled a deep breath. He could have stayed away from Liv, but the truth was, he was eager to catch up with her without the girls overhearing.

He had been a year ahead of her in school and they had known each other most of their lives. They'd dated for almost two years before she'd become pregnant, and Zane had always thought he'd marry her. But after they found out about Miley, her parents had forbidden her from seeing him, and she hadn't fought them. They pulled her out of school and she spent the rest of the year homeschooling. Very few people in Marshall even knew Liv had been pregnant and even fewer knew he was the father. The last time he saw her was the day Miley was born.

He had often wondered about her, but he'd honored her parents' wishes. After he met Tanya, he wanted to honor his marriage, too. She had asked about Liv a few times but was happy enough to leave the past behind them.

Zane walked into the commercial kitchen and found Liv standing near the large stove, several pots bubbling and steaming on the burners.

She stood with one hand on her hip while the other stirred something in a pot. She didn't look frenzied or hurried, but her eyebrows came together in a little frown and she worried her bottom lip.

He took the opportunity to just watch her for a minute. She'd changed a bit over the past eleven years, turning from a tall, lanky youth into a tall, elegant woman. He had so many questions for her but wondered how much she wanted to share. He could almost see the shield she wore around her heart and had thrown up several times while they spoke earlier. She had probably spent the past decade using it to protect herself from pain.

He wondered if she also used it to keep people out.

She looked up and jumped at the sight of him, putting her hand over her heart.

"Sorry," he said. "I didn't mean to scare you."

A timer went off and she grabbed two oven mitts. "It's okay. I'm just a little jumpy tonight." She removed a pan of garlic bread from the oven and set it on a stainless-steel counter.

"Do you need help?" He joined her near the stove. "It smells amazing."

"Just spaghetti and meatballs." She shrugged and turned down the burner under the sauce. "I hope your girls like spaghetti."

"They'd live off it if I let them."

She smiled and set a colander in the sink. "Good."

"Here, let me help." He took the oven mitts from her and removed the boiling spaghetti off the stove.

Liv stood back and let him drain the noodles. "Thanks." She watched him for a second and then went to a rack and removed some plates. "I spoke to my parents, and they don't think they can get here for a couple more days. I hope that's okay."

He finished draining the noodles and replaced them in the pot, a little relieved that he wouldn't have to face her parents quite yet. "I completely understand. I'm just happy the girls and I were able to make it before the roads got too bad."

"So am I."

He set the pot of noodles on the counter. "I'll have plenty of time to see the resort while we're here. When your parents arrive, I can interview them—after Christmas, of course. We're not in any hurry." He leaned against the counter and tossed the mitts aside. "Did you tell them who I am?"

She was busy arranging the garlic bread in a basket. "I did."

"What about Miley?"

There was a slight pause in her movements,

and then she set the last piece of bread in the basket and wiped her hands on a towel. "I told them about her, too."

He held his breath.

"They were surprised, as you can imagine." She finally turned to look at him. "But it'll be okay."

Something in the tone of her voice told him things weren't quite okay, but he knew Liv would do her best to smooth things over.

"Let's see," she said. "What else will we need?"

"How are you doing, Liv?"

She paused. "What do you mean?"

"How have you been since—"

"Since Miley was born?" She picked up the dish towel and folded it absently. "I won't lie. It's been really hard."

"Where did you go? What happened to you?"

"I went to live with my aunt and uncle in Timber Falls and spent my senior year there." She set the towel down again and crossed her arms. "I made some really good friends and tried hard to pretend everything was normal."

"No one knew?"

She shook her head. "I've never told anyone. Not even my best friend, Piper."

"Wow. That's a lot to carry by yourself."

"It was the hardest thing I've ever done." She played with a loose thread on her scarf. "It feels strange to openly talk about Miley after eleven years of keeping it all to myself."

The last thing he wanted to do was hurt her further. "Are you okay with all of it?"

A slow smile lifted her lips. "It's good, Zane. I never thought I'd meet her, and now I get to spend Christmas with her. I'm still pinching myself. I know it might not be easy," she said quickly, "but I want to get to know her more than anything in the world." She gently tilted her head. "And getting to know Alexis is a wonderful bonus. I'm looking forward to spending time with both the girls."

"What about me?" The question slipped out before he even considered the implications and immediately he wished he could reel it back in. "Sorry—"

"It's okay." She clasped her hands in front of her and nodded. "I'm looking forward to spending time with you, too."

"Even after all we've been through?"

"Especially after all we've been through." Her face softened. "We have some good memories mixed in with the hard ones. If anyone understands what the past eleven years have been like, it's you. It's nice to have someone to finally talk with about her."

He couldn't imagine what the past eleven years would have been like without Miley in his life. He hurt for Liv and all she'd lost.

"I have pictures," he said as he pulled his phone from his pocket. "Would you like to see some?"

Liv nodded. "I'd love to."

She joined him as he opened his picture app. She smelled like fresh flowers and when she stood so close to him, every one of his senses came alive, though he had to push back the feelings.

He hadn't dated since Tanya's death, choosing, instead, to focus on being a dad. He couldn't take the risk of opening his heart to Liv again. There was too much past hurt between them and too much present confusion and uncertainty.

Besides, he wasn't deluding himself. Once her family arrived, any sort of peace or understanding he and Liv had found would be muddled and become more complicated.

Family always had a way of getting involved. And if her family was anything like he remembered, he was in for some serious battles.

But he'd do it all for Miley. For better or worse, she deserved to know her family— especially her mom.

For now, he'd just focus on the next two days. There were eleven years of catching up, and he planned to make the bridge between Liv and Miley as smooth as possible— at least, until her family showed up.

Chapter Four

The first thing Liv thought about the next morning when her eyes opened was Miley. Yesterday felt like a dream—an unexpected and amazing dream. Had she truly met her daughter, after all this time? It didn't seem possible, yet it was true. The perfect Christmas surprise. And now she had a full day to spend with Miley, Alexis and Zane before her family arrived. The night before, they had laughed and visited around the small kitchen table, eating spaghetti and meatballs, but the girls had been tired from a long day of traveling. Everyone had gone to bed early.

But today was a new day, full of bright sunshine and the most brilliant blue sky Liv had ever seen. She hurried through her morning routine, marveling at how everything looked more vibrant today than the day before. There was a lightness to her heart that hadn't been there in a long, long time. It brought a smile to her lips and a shine to her eyes that surprised her when she looked in the mirror.

She took a little extra time with her appearance, trying not to wonder what Zane thought about her, eleven years older, with the careworn wrinkles just starting to crease near her eyes. She put on a pair of cropped jeans and an oversize sweater with a thick cowl neck, leaving her hair down with a little curl to it.

Before Zane and the girls could wake up, she wanted to have breakfast ready. There was so much to do today, and she didn't want to waste time cooking while they waited for her.

The lodge was quiet as she walked down the stairs to the dining room, but a very distinct smell met her nose before she put her foot on the last step.

It was coffee and something sweet. Pancakes?

Liv stared in disbelief when she entered the kitchen. Zane was at the stove, flipping pancakes, her mother's apron tied around his waist, while Miley and Alexis set the table. Their faces were bright and their damp hair was braided in matching rows down the sides of their heads. Had Zane braided their hair?

The idea made her widen her smile. Miley was dressed in a sweater and blue jeans, while Alexis wore red-and-black-checkered pants, a purple shirt and a red cape. At the ends of her braids were purple ribbons. Both wore slippers.

Everyone looked as if they belonged in this kitchen, like family, instead of guests.

A longing Liv had buried deep in her heart suddenly burst forth with a pounding urgency she didn't expect. She placed her hand on her chest, afraid the thud it made against her breastbone would be heard by the three who bustled about the kitchen.

This was what her heart had longed for, yet what she'd denied herself over and over again. For years, she had watched her brothers and friends grow their families, and while she had lived alone, cooking, cleaning and planning for just one, she had known this simple scene was playing out in the homes of her loved ones on a daily basis. Yet she had given up this chance when she handed Miley over to the social worker.

Miley fussed at Alexis for putting two spoons next to a plate, and Alexis fussed back that she didn't have another fork. Zane glanced at the girls, probably to see what the squabble was about, but he caught Liv's gaze instead and offered her a warm, dazzling smile. His glasses made him look a bit scholarly, though the apron said otherwise.

"Good morning," he said. "We had hoped to finish before you came down."

"Morning!" Miley called out to Liv. She and Alexis left the table and rushed across the kitchen to embrace Liv in a tight hug.

Liv's mouth parted as she looked down at their shining faces, so full of excitement and acceptance.

And she remembered the moment she had given Miley away. She would never have believed that eleven years later, Miley would willingly come back.

But what if Miley knew that Liv had abandoned her? Would she be so eager to accept her now?

"Do you like pancakes?" Miley asked, wholly unaware of the turmoil in Liv's heart.

"They're my favorite," Alexis said. "Daddy makes them with chocolate chips for me and blueberries for Miley."

"I didn't ask you," Miley pointed out to Alexis. "I asked Liv."

It took Liv a second to compose herself as she returned the girls' hugs.

Zane stood by, a spatula in hand, as he watched his daughters with Liv. He smiled at Liv again, and she wondered how her heart would survive this onslaught of affection and emotions.

"Okay, girls," Zane said. "Let Liv have a little space." He offered Liv an apologetic shrug. "They've spent most of their lives moving from one place to the next, and they seem to attach quickly to people they really like."

The girls grinned up at Liv, almost as if telling her they *did* like her and were agreeing with their father. But Liv couldn't shake the fear that if Miley knew the truth, she wouldn't be so happy to extend her affection.

"*Do* you like pancakes?" Miley asked, her blue eyes hopeful. "Because Daddy made a *lot* of them."

Again, Zane offered that apologetic shrug as he motioned toward two large stacks of pancakes, steaming on the counter next to him. "My internal clock is all messed up, so I've been awake for a couple of hours. I didn't know what else to do with myself."

"I love pancakes," Liv said, her heart finally returning to its regular rhythm.

"Which ones do you like best?" Alexis asked. "Chocolate chips." She grinned. "Or blueberries?" She scrunched up her nose in disapproval.

Miley watched Liv closely, her gaze hopeful.

Liv threw up her hands. "I love them both equally."

The girls laughed, and Zane nodded his approval as he turned back to the stove and flipped another pancake.

A few minutes later, Zane and the girls laughed and teased one another as they dished up their pancakes. Liv watched in quiet wonder at the love these three shared. What a gift family was—a gift she hadn't appreciated when she was a child, and one she had been keenly aware of missing as an adult. Even though these two little girls had lost their mother, it was clear that Zane had done an amazing job as their sole parent. Not only were the girls curious and smart, they were confident and comfortable to be around. Their stories about life in Berlin, Paris, London and a host of other foreign cities were amazing to Liv. How many eleven- and five-year-old children had seen as much as these two?

All too soon, breakfast was done and the dishes were washed. The morning had slipped past without Liv's notice.

"Have you ever been skating?" Liv asked the girls as she tossed the drying rag on the counter.

"Ice skating?" Miley asked.

"Yes. There's a spot on the lake designated for skating." Liv walked with them out of the kitchen and turned off the light. The large dining room was bright with sunshine glinting off the fresh snow outside the large windows.

"No!" Miley exclaimed. "But we don't have skates."

"There are several pairs in the warming house down by the lake," Liv said. "I'm sure we'll find some to fit you and Alexis."

"Let's hurry and get on our outdoor clothes," Zane suggested to the girls.

Ten minutes later, they were cutting a path through the knee-deep snow on their way to the lake. Though the sky was clear and the sun was bright, it was freezing. Little ice crystals danced in the air, reflecting the sun, offering a breathtaking remnant of yesterday's storm.

"I hope you're ready to do a little work," Liv called to Zane and the girls. "If my dad was here, he would have shoveled the fresh snow off the lake by now. He marked off the skating section last week and cleaned up the ice once already."

"Does your dad still skate?" Zane asked,

no doubt recalling Bob Butler's fame as a hockey player.

"Not as much as he'd like." Liv glanced back at Zane, a smile tugging up her cold cheeks. Her dad had been playing hockey for the University of Minnesota when he had been drafted to play in the NHL. But an injury during his first game left him partially blind in his right eye and his dreams of a professional hockey career had died. He'd married Liv's mom, moved to Marshall to work for the city and they had started their family. He coached their high school hockey team and had taken them to State a few times. He lived and breathed hockey, as did Liv's two brothers and their kids. "But it's still a Butler family tradition."

"I remember it quite well." Zane chuckled.

"You weren't much of a hockey player, if I remember." Liv trudged through the snow, growing nice and warm from the effort. Thankfully, it was soft and light, or it would have taken a lot more work to break the path.

"No." Zane shook his head. "I wasn't into hockey. Basketball was a much warmer sport."

Liv smiled to herself. She had forgotten the deep rift it had caused in her family when she'd started to date Zane—one of their high school basketball stars. Since the hockey and basketball seasons coincided, often with games and matches on the same night, she usually opted to attend Zane's games over her brothers' matches. Her mom had been disappointed with her, her father hurt and her brothers angry. Butlers Stick Together was their mantra. It had been one of the first times Liv had gone against the wishes of her family, and no one liked it.

"I sure hope your brothers have moved past their rivalry," Zane said, almost to himself. "The hockey players and basketball players didn't intermingle much."

"That's an understatement." A niggle of doubt pushed its way into Liv's good mood. Her brothers were big, loud and overbearing at the best of times. They hadn't liked Zane much as teenagers. What made her think they'd like him any more now? One of them was the new head coach of the Marshall hockey team and the other managed the ice arena. They didn't leave Minnesota often, and when they did, it wasn't to travel to places like Dublin, Berlin and Paris. Would they even have anything in common with Zane?

The holidays ahead started to look more and more daunting. Maybe it wasn't such a good idea to have Zane stay with the girls.

Now that they were reconnected, they could meet up somewhere less volatile.

But what about the magazine article? If it wasn't written, Zane's chance at working for the magazine might be threatened.

"Daddy," Miley said as she walked behind Zane. "Do you know Liv's family?"

Liv stopped in her tracks, the lake not too far away. Zane also stopped, his brown-eyed gaze catching on Liv's.

What would he tell Miley? Of course she would want to know. Liv was a stranger to her, yet it sounded as if her father knew her well.

"I do know Liv's family," Zane said, putting his hand on Miley's stocking cap. "I went to school with Liv and her brothers in Marshall, where we all grew up."

Miley's blue eyes opened wide with surprise and delight. "You were friends?"

Zane glanced at Liv again, his eyes warm as he smiled. "I was good friends with Liv."

"Look," Miley said, pointing to the lake, apparently satisfied with the answer and ready to move on. "Is that where we're going to skate?"

Liv looked in the direction and nodded, feeling a bit like she'd been whiplashed from one topic to the next. "Yes. Do you see the orange cones with the flags? Those are the four corners of the skating rink. Ready to shovel some snow?"

Miley and Alexis cheered as they jumped up and down.

A warming house stood close to the lake. Liv opened the door and took out four snow shovels. For the next twenty minutes, they pushed the snow off the ice until it was ready for skating.

Liv helped Alexis tie her skates while Zane helped Miley. The girls chatted almost non-stop, their cheeks pink from the cool air. Within minutes, Miley and Alexis were skating around the ice, as if they'd been doing it all their lives.

Liv had grown up skating but hadn't done it for a few years. She felt a little wobbly on her feet as she and Zane stepped onto the ice. She started to fall and grabbed on to his arm on instinct.

"Sorry." She pulled her hand away, embarrassed that she had been so familiar with him.

"It's okay." He winked at her. "I might need to reach out to you for a little support before this is done."

She met his smile, knowing he was teasing but wondering if he was still talking about ice skating.

"You're doing great with Miley," he said, quiet enough that Miley couldn't hear from her spot across the ice rink.

"Am I?" Liv let out a breath she hadn't known she'd been holding. "I feel so self-conscious around her. I know she's not judging me—probably isn't even giving me much thought—but—"

"That's where you're wrong." Zane stood next to Liv as they watched the girls laughing and playing on the ice. "I can tell she really likes you, and she's very conscious of you. See." He nodded toward Miley who cast Liv a glance after she tried a spin on the ice. "She's looking to see if you're watching her skate. I can see the respect and admiration she has for you. Even if she doesn't realize it, she's looking for your approval."

"My approval? I mean nothing to her."

"That's not true." Zane shook his head. "You're a beautiful, stylish and interesting woman who loves ballet. She looks up to you."

Zane still thought she was beautiful? Liv's cheeks warmed, but she pushed aside his compliment. He was probably speaking in generalities.

Nevertheless, she stood up a little taller and

smiled at Miley, nodding encouragement to the girl.

Miley grinned and then did the spin again.

"Kids are some of our biggest cheerleaders—and our harshest critics." Zane chuckled. "But it's good to remember they're watching our every step."

"That's a little daunting."

"Maybe." He shrugged. "But I can guarantee that you have nothing to worry about. You're a pretty amazing woman, Liv Butler. Miley would be fortunate to grow up and be just like you."

For the first time that day, a heavy weight settled in Liv's gut.

That was the last thing she wanted for her daughter.

The day went by way too fast for Zane, and before he knew it, they were sitting around the fireplace in the main lodge, their stomachs full from homemade pizza, and their cheeks pink from being outside for most of the day.

Liv sat next to a coffee table on the floor with Miley to her right and Alexis to her left. Her back was toward the fireplace, and the blazing flames offered a soft glow to her hair.

Zane sat across from her and didn't say much as he watched her and the girls interact.

It was obvious that the girls really liked Liv. They hadn't left her side all day, and it appeared that their fascination with her was mutual. Liv's eyes shone and her cheeks were rosy as she answered their questions and asked a few of her own. Zane appreciated that she didn't single out Miley's company, but paid just as much attention to Alexis. Neither girl would have any reason to believe Liv favored one over the other.

"Are you getting tired?" Liv asked Zane as she met his gaze. A board game was spread out on the coffee table between them, but he had little interest in playing. He was having a much better time just watching Liv and the girls together.

"No." He shook his head. "Just being a bit sentimental."

Liv smiled and he was struck anew by her beauty. He'd never met a more confident woman. But it was more than her looks that attracted him to her. She was so conscious of the people around her—always on alert to their needs and feelings. Her kindness came so naturally. He couldn't help but wonder why she had never married, then he realized he didn't actually know if she had ever married.

She hadn't mentioned a husband or boyfriend, but that didn't mean there wasn't one. Maybe she *did* have someone serious in her life.

Suddenly, it was the only thing Zane could think about. Was she in a relationship?

He tried to tell himself his interest had to do with Miley and not himself. If Liv was dating or married, then that man would have a profound impact on Miley's life once they told her the truth. Shouldn't Zane be concerned about who that man might be? Didn't he have a right to know?

But now wasn't the time to talk about significant others—not around the girls. Besides, Alexis's eyes were starting to droop, and Miley had tried hard to cover her yawns. The girls had played hard all day and were exhausted.

"We should probably think about getting to bed," Zane said, surprised to hear the disappointment in his voice.

"Not yet, Daddy," Miley protested. "We're not done with our game."

"This could take several more hours," Liv said in a gentle voice. "We'll have plenty of time to finish it while you're here."

"Daddy," Miley said, "you don't look tired."

Zane wasn't tired, surprisingly. He hadn't felt this energetic or invigorated for a long time. Just being in Liv's presence again had made him feel younger. It wasn't often that he met a woman with as much energy and enthusiasm for the outdoors as her. It had been years since he'd played in the snow all day. "I'm not tired, but that doesn't mean you and Alexis shouldn't get some sleep." He started to rise, but Miley put her hand on his shoulder.

"I'll take Alexis to bed," Miley said, sounding a lot older than her eleven years. "I'll help her get into her pajamas and read her a story."

Alexis grinned, obviously liking the idea of her sister reading to her. Miley didn't make the offer often, but when she did, it always made Alexis happy.

And Zane wasn't about to ruin it for the two of them. "Okay. I'll be up in a minute to check on you."

"Don't worry about us," Miley said, standing up and motioning for Alexis to follow her. "We'll be fine. You can stay here for as long as you like."

The girls giggled and sent sly glances in Liv's direction.

Apparently, they were trying to play matchmaker.

Zane should correct them and put their girlish dreams to rest, but there was a part of him that was thankful they were ready to see him with another woman. They hadn't even asked him if he was going to date again since their mom died. The notion that they wanted to play matchmaker gave him some hope that they were healing and moving on.

Yet, when Zane met Liv's gaze across the table, and saw the uncertainty in her eyes, he knew he should probably have a chat with his daughters and let them know not to interfere. His opportunity to be with Liv had come and gone eleven years ago. Too much time and hurt had passed between them. Besides, he had no interest in a romantic relationship now or in the future. The girls were his life now. He needed to put all his energy and time into raising them.

The best he could offer Miley and Alexis was a good friendship with Liv. Which was something he could tell would come easily. It always had. Even when they had dated in high school, their friendship had been strong. When they had left Marshall, he had not only lost his girlfriend, he'd lost his best friend.

"Good night," Zane said as the girls came up to him for their nightly hugs. "I'll be in to pray for you in a little bit."

Miley hugged Zane. "Take your time."

She then went to Liv and said, "May I hug you good-night?"

Liv's eyes lit up and a gentle smile tugged at the corners of her lips. "Of course."

Miley fell into Liv's arms and squeezed her tight.

Closing her eyes, Liv hugged Miley back. She pressed her lips together, almost as if she was trying to stop them from trembling.

"Good night," Miley said.

"Good night." Liv opened her eyes again and blinked several times. Then it was Alexis's turn for a hug before the girls ran up the steps, Alexis's red cape flying behind her.

When Zane looked back at Liv, she was staring down at the board game, her hand up near her lips.

"I can't tell you how many times today I've had to hide my emotions from those girls," she finally said, her voice low and soft. "Every time I turn around, they're lavishing me with their love and attention. I'm not used to it."

"They're good girls." Zane couldn't conceal the hint of pride that colored his words.

"Very good." Liv folded her arms on the coffee table in front of her. "You're a really great dad, Zane. They're blessed to have you."

"Thank you." Her words warmed his heart,

though he knew he could easily tell her all the ways he was failing his daughters. All the guilt that plagued him from carting them around the world to pursue his career, when they should have had a steady school and a familiar backyard to play in.

He didn't want to talk about any of that right now. Instead, he wanted to know more about Liv. His earlier questions nagged at his thoughts. Was Liv in a relationship? Did he have a right to know—as Miley's dad?

"What about you?" he asked. "Did you ever think about having more kids?"

She left the floor and took a seat, pulling her legs up onto the chair. There was a sad smile on her lips. "I'm not cut out to be a mom."

Zane frowned. Everything he knew about Liv was in stark contrast to her statement. Not only was she really good with his girls, but she had all the qualities a mom needed. Patience, maturity, kindness, love, courage, strength. The list went on and on. "What do you mean?"

"You saw how easily I gave up Miley." She nodded toward the stairs where the girls had just left, her entire body growing rigid. "I didn't put up a fight when they took her away from me. What kind of a mom does that?"

She took one of the playing pieces off the board and toyed with it between her fingers. "Why would God entrust another child to me when I didn't want the one He gave me?"

The fire popped and a log split in two, sending a cascade of sparks up the chimney, but Zane just stared at Liv. Did she really believe what she was saying?

"Liv, I know those things aren't true. Just seeing you with Miley tells me a lot about you and what you actually wanted—but maybe didn't know how to fight for at the age of seventeen." He leaned forward and put his elbows on his knees. "You would make a great mom." He couldn't even believe he had to tell her that. "You are one of the kindest, most caring people I've ever known."

She lowered her gaze, embarrassment tingeing her voice. "I'm not trying to sound sorry for myself or trying to get you to pay me a compliment." She paused. "I guess the easier answer to your question would have been that I never found anyone I wanted to create a family with."

The fire continued to crackle as the room started to feel closer and more intimate. He'd never felt so far removed from the rest of the world as he did now. "So…there's no one?"

Liv shook her head. "Not for a while." She

lifted a shoulder and continued to play with the game piece. "It's easier that way. I've been so busy this year, working on this place and running my businesses. In a way, I feel married to my work."

"That can be rewarding, too." Zane could understand how easy it would be to fall headfirst into his work if he didn't have the girls to balance out his life.

She gave him a look. "Not quite the same thing, I know. But, I'm proud of the businesses I've grown."

"And you should be." Zane couldn't deny that he was relieved she was single. It would make things less messy with Miley.

At least, that's what he told himself.

He couldn't admit that he was relieved for his own sake, as well.

Chapter Five

There were just three days left before Christmas and with Liv's mom gone, there were no more cookies to be had. Liv stood in the kitchen with Miley and Alexis on either side of her the next afternoon as the three of them added ingredients to a large mixing bowl.

"Can I pour in the flour, yet?" Alexis asked, her little feet moving impatiently on the stool Liv had pulled up to the counter. She wore a pair of red sequined shoes and a black dress with a yellow shirt underneath. Liv looked forward to seeing what she would wear each day.

"Not yet," Liv said. "We need to get all the wet ingredients added before we put the dry ones in."

"Wet ingredients?" Miley asked. "What are those?"

Liv smiled as she added the eggs the girls had already cracked into a separate bowl. "The ones that make the dough sticky, like the butter and eggs."

It was just Liv and the girls in the kitchen. Zane had stayed in his room to catch up on some emails. Liv appreciated the time alone with the girls. They were open and comfortable around their dad, but there was something extra special about girl time. At least, that's what Miley had told her when they started to bake.

"Do you have a husband, Liv?" Miley asked as she put the sugar into the mixing bowl.

The question was unexpected and Liv paused as she scraped the edge of the bowl with the rubber spatula. "No."

"No kids, either?" Alexis asked, the cup of flour poised and ready in her small hand. Her face was innocent as she studied Liv.

Liv glanced at Miley, wishing for all the world that she could claim her as her own, but she had no right. "No, I don't."

"Hmm." Miley put down the empty measuring cup and rested her face in her hand. "My dad's not married, but he said we can't ask you to be his wife."

Liv's mouth slipped open in surprise. "He talked to you about this?"

"He said he doesn't want you as his wife." Miley sighed. "So we can't have you as our mom."

Alexis's mouth turned down and Miley's bottom lip puckered out.

Zane didn't want her as his wife? The statement hurt worse than it should, since she had no desire to be his wife—had not even contemplated such a thing. Yet knowing how he felt was like a blow to her gut, and pride, for some reason.

"Your dad and I are friends," Liv managed to say. "We're not supposed to be husband and wife."

"Husbands and wives aren't friends?" Alexis's face looked so sad, Liv wanted to ease her little heart.

"Of course they're friends," she clarified quickly. "They should be the very best of friends."

Miley's eyes lit up. "Then you and Daddy can get married, since you're already friends."

"It doesn't work like that." Liv suddenly felt overly warm. How had this conversation started? And, better yet, how could she get it to end? "Husbands and wives are a special kind of friendship. It's called a romantic friendship. That's not the kind of friendship your dad and I have."

"So you don't want to marry him, either?" Miley's eyebrows came together.

Liv wiped her hands on the white apron she had tied around her waist and moved away from the counter to get the baking powder. She didn't want to say anything that might get misinterpreted by the girls and repeated to Zane. No doubt they had misunderstood whatever he had said to them—though the message was clear to Liv. The girls were trying to play matchmaker and he had set them straight. She appreciated his efforts, but it looked like she would need to address it, too.

She grabbed the baking powder and went back to the girls, who were watching her for her answer. "Your dad and I wouldn't be good as husband and wife." She shook her head and tried to reassure them with a smile. "I don't think I'll ever get married."

"Don't you like our daddy?" Alexis asked.

"Of course I like your daddy. Just not in the way a wife should like her husband."

"Hi, Daddy," Alexis said, a smile lighting up her face.

Liv lifted her head and she found Zane standing in the doorway. How long had he been there? And what had he heard?

He met Liv's gaze but gave no indication either way.

There was nothing for Liv to do but smile and try to cover her embarrassment. "You're just in time. We're almost ready to roll out the cookies."

"It sounds like you're having a pretty serious conversation." He moved into the kitchen, his careful gaze on Liv's face. "Do you need me to intervene?"

"I don't think so." Liv smiled at the girls. "I think we've said all that needs to be said."

"Liv likes you, Daddy," Alexis said with a disappointed and dramatic sigh. "She just doesn't think you'd be a good husband."

"That's not what I said—" Liv stopped herself, knowing she could never make him understand what she meant.

Zane's gaze didn't leave Liv's face and his feelings were hard to read within his eyes. "Well," he finally said. "I guess that's settled."

Liv let out a breath. Maybe she could clarify things later, or maybe she should just let them be.

"What can I do to help with these cookies?" he asked as he moved Miley's blond hair off her shoulder. The girls' hair was crinkled from their braids yesterday and Miley was wearing hers with a simple red headband.

They worked for several minutes to get the

dough ready. Zane floured the counter, and Liv helped the girls with the heavy wooden roller to spread it out.

When they were finally ready to start cutting out the shapes, Liv was so engrossed in their work that she didn't notice the two new arrivals at the kitchen door until Zane went completely still.

Mom and Dad stood just inside the kitchen wearing their winter coats and hats, snow clinging to their boots.

Miley and Alexis stopped cutting out cookies and just stared.

"Mom," Liv said, wiping her hands on her apron as she moved away from the counter. "Dad." She smiled, forcing herself to stay calm. "You made it back much earlier than I anticipated."

Mom's face was hard as she stared at Miley.

The little girl was adorable with a smudge of flour on her cheek and white fingerprints on her red sweater. But did her mom think so? The look on her face was not one of pleasure or joy at seeing her granddaughter for the first time since her birth.

Zane took a step closer to Miley, whether on purpose or instinct, Liv wasn't sure.

"We thought it best to brave the roads,"

Dad said to Liv. "We didn't think it was right to leave you alone with our guests."

"That's just silly." Liv tried to make her voice sound light and playful. "We were having a marvelous time without you."

"I can see that." Mom finally looked at Zane and lifted her chin. "We didn't expect to see you again. Not after what happened."

"Mom." Liv couldn't risk her mom saying something inappropriate in front of Miley. She took a step toward her, almost to shield Miley and Zane. "Why don't we save that conversation for another time? I'd like you to meet Zane's daughters. They were so surprised to learn that Zane already knew our family." She tried to give her mom a pleading look. "They're the sweetest children you'll ever meet. I hope you can enjoy their company while they're here and save any conversation you feel you need to have with their father for a different time and place."

Dad put his hand on Mom's arm, like he'd done a hundred times before. He was giving her a physical reminder to calm herself. Out of everyone involved eleven years ago, it was Mom who had been the most upset and hurt by Liv. Appearances meant everything to her and having her daughter shame her with a teenage pregnancy had been one of the worst things Liv could have done. Mom had forced Liv to stay home for months, only leaving for her doctor's appointments in another town.

Mom's hazel eyes were leveled on Liv, but she gave her the slightest nod and then put a fake smile on her face. She moved around Liv to join Zane and his daughters at the counter. "Hello," she said, her tone a little more pleasant though very formal. "Thank you for joining us. We hope you have everything you need."

Liv looked to her father, but he just gave her a gentle shrug. Though he supported his wife through thick and thin, he had always been one of Liv's biggest allies. He tempered her mother like no one else could, but he had his limits.

He moved around Liv and extended his hand to Zane. "Welcome to Lakepoint Lodge, Zane. It's nice to see you again." He smiled and it looked much more genuine than Mom's. "And these are your daughters?"

Zane nodded, his gaze leery as he looked between Mom and Dad. He put his arm around Miley and said, "This is Miley."

Mom and Dad stared at Miley and Liv wondered what they were thinking. Did they see the resemblance between her and her daughter? Did they see how much her blue eyes matched Liv's?

"Hello, Miley." Dad nodded at her. "It's nice to finally meet you."

"Hello." Miley was so much more reserved than she had been since Liv had met her two days ago. She looked at Mom, but Mom did not offer her a smile.

"And this is my youngest, Alexis," Zane said, reaching out to put his hand on Alexis's shoulder.

"I'm five," Alexis said, holding up five doughy fingers.

"Hi, Alexis," Dad said.

Mom didn't say anything else to anyone, but turned and left the kitchen.

Dad took off his hat, his white hair in wild disarray. To his credit, he looked a little embarrassed by Mom's behavior. "Marilyn and I will haul in our things and put everything away. We'll give you some time to finish up the cookies. We can chat about the, ah, article later. Maybe when we have a little more privacy. How does that sound?"

Liv knew he didn't really mean the article but was thankful he wasn't more specific around the girls.

"I think that's a good idea," Zane said, his

countenance heavy. "I'm sure there are a lot of things you'd like to know."

Dad pressed his lips together and nodded. He placed his hand on Zane's shoulder and patted it in a familiar way. "It's nice to see you again, Zane. And real nice to meet your family."

"It's nice to see you again, too, Mr. Butler."

"Just call me Bob," he said. "Same as everyone else."

Dad offered Liv a sad smile and then left the kitchen.

"I'm sorry," Liv said to Zane, rejoining him at the counter. "Maybe this wasn't such a good idea."

"We'll get it figured out." Zane handed Miley one of the cookie cutters. "It had to happen eventually."

The girls watched them for a second and then went back to their cookies, oblivious to the drama that had just unfolded around them—and the trouble that was yet to come.

Liv wished she had the same luxury.

An hour later, Zane closed the door to his suite, his chest heavy with all the things left unsaid in the kitchen. He had brought Miley and Alexis up to their room for a rest and told them to hang out there until he came back to get them. The last thing he needed was for one of them to come looking for him and overhear what he knew would be a heated and passionate discussion with Liv's parents. Ideally, he'd wait until later when they were in bed to have the conversation, but he didn't think it wise to go that long without confronting the situation.

He walked down the hall toward the stairs, wishing this conversation didn't have to happen but knowing it was long overdue. For years, he didn't think the Butlers deserved to know what had happened to Miley, but time and maturity had helped him to see that they had made choices out of fear and concern for their daughter. Maybe enough time had passed for them to realize what they had missed.

Liv stood near the fireplace in the main room, staring into the flames. She looked so lonely standing there, like she had the weight of both their troubles pressed upon her shoulders. For the past eleven years, he'd thought of Miley as the victim in this situation, but spending just two days in Liv's company made him realize she had suffered far more than anyone. He longed to heal the broken places in her heart that had shattered the day she gave Miley away. But how? Could anything heal a hurt like that?

She turned and the smile that had been playing about her face for the past couple of days was gone. There was no more shine to her eyes or glow in her cheeks. After two days of joy, reality had come knocking on their door.

"I'm sorry, Zane. My mom—"

"You don't need to apologize for her. I know she's angry at me, but that has nothing to do with you. I'm sure she has a lot of questions."

"I doubt she'll even listen to you. She's already convinced herself of the worst possible scenario and that's what she's—"

He put his hand on her forearm. "Let's give her the benefit of the doubt."

She looked down at his hand, but she didn't pull away. Instead, she put her free hand on top of his. "Thank you for being so understanding."

Her voice was warm and soft, and her touch sent a rush of sensations racing up his arm, right into his chest.

How did she still have the ability to completely undo him? Nothing else existed in this moment except for Liv Butler. He looked into her beautiful blue eyes and was lost—

completely lost. Dozens of memories from their high school years rushed up and filled his mind with easier times and places. What would have happened had they not made such poor choices that night after homecoming? Would their relationship have grown and matured into something deeper—something permanent?

But those thoughts were futile, because if they had made other choices, then Miley and Alexis wouldn't be a part of his life. He couldn't even imagine something like that. His girls meant everything to him. He would do anything for them, even relive all the heartbreak and pain from the past eleven years.

The look in Liv's eyes shifted, and she pulled away from his touch. "I suppose there's no way to avoid this." She squared her shoulders and took a deep breath.

"At least we're doing this together. Finally." He hadn't been with her when she told her parents that she was pregnant. There hadn't been a chance for him to talk to her mom and dad after they found out the truth. They'd forbidden her from seeing him or talking to him again. Every decision made was communicated between their parents. The only time they'd seen each other again was that day at the hospital when Miley was born, but God had still found a way to bring them to this point.

Liv motioned toward a door at the back of the room near the long desk. "They're in their private quarters."

Zane followed her and stood behind her as she knocked.

"Come in," her dad called out. At least Bob was civil. Zane just hoped Marilyn had been given enough time to cool off.

Liv gave Zane one last look before opening the door.

The private quarters were much larger than Zane had expected. An oversize living room had massive windows looking out into the pine trees behind the lodge. An open kitchen was in one corner and two doors led off to the right and to the left. Pine-plank floors, thick pine trim and plush furniture made the room warm and inviting. A small fireplace, similar to the one in the main room, blazed to the right.

Bob and Marilyn Butler sat on one of the sofas flanking the fireplace. When Liv and Zane entered, Bob stood.

"Come on in," he said to them. "Marilyn and I have been waiting for you."

Despite the fact that Zane had spent the

past eleven years turning into a man, he felt like an inexperienced eighteen-year-old boy again. His heart pounded and he had to swallow a few times to make sure his voice would work properly.

Marilyn made no move to welcome them or invite them in. She just stared at the fire, her arms and legs crossed.

Liv glanced at Zane and tried to smile. She took a seat on the sofa opposite from her parents and he sat next to her, drawing strength from her presence.

For the first time in eleven years, he didn't feel like he was facing this battle alone. He and Liv were now in this together, and the truth of that realization gave him a boost of energy and courage. It also created a wave of affection for Liv. Every last shred of hurt or resentment he'd felt for her these past eleven years melted away.

Liv was Miley's mother, and she was putting herself in the line of fire to protect her daughter.

No one said anything for a moment, and then Liv finally leaned forward.

"Mom, I know you're upset—"

"You have no idea how I feel, Olivia." Marilyn finally looked at Liv. Her face was a mask, and the only emotion she revealed was anger. She looked at Zane. "I can't believe you would do this to us."

Zane frowned.

"What has Zane done?" Liv asked.

"He came here, knowing full well who we were, and planned to foist his child upon us."

Liv clenched her hands on her lap and Zane's back went rigid. "I had no idea who you were," he said. "I didn't have any clue until I saw Liv in the parking lot. And I would never *foist* Miley on anyone."

"Now, Marilyn," Bob said, putting his hand on her knee. "These things just happen."

"What are the chances?" Marilyn asked Bob, pulling her knee away from his touch. "Just think about it."

"Mom." Liv moved forward on the couch. "This was a complete surprise to both of us, and we're trying to make the best of this situation. Zane wants nothing from us, though, in my opinion, he deserves more than we can give him."

"What about you?" Marilyn asked her daughter. "I can't imagine what kind of havoc this is playing on your emotions and mental well-being."

"Havoc?" Liv's voice lowered. "Meeting Miley is the best thing that's ever happened to me. For the past eleven years, my emotions and mental well-being have been in havoc. It wasn't until I actually met her that I've felt any semblance of peace about what happened, though the guilt and shame I feel will be a part of me for the rest of my life."

"Is this what you wanted to hear?" Marilyn asked Zane. "Did you want to see the pain and anguish you've caused in Liv's life?"

Zane opened his mouth to defend himself, but Liv put her hand on his arm.

"Zane has nothing to do with my pain or anguish—neither does Miley. If there's anyone to blame for the torment I've lived these past eleven years, it's me."

Her hand remained on his arm and he wanted to reach out and take it in his own, to offer her some sort of comfort or strength, but refrained.

"Liv." Bob leaned forward. "We just want what's best for you."

"No, you don't." She shook her head. "You've always wanted what was best for you. You never once asked me what I wanted."

"What did you want?" Marilyn asked. "More pain and heartache?"

"I wanted my baby." Liv's voice cracked and tears filled her eyes. "I wanted a chance to know her—even if I couldn't raise her— and Zane has offered me that chance." She looked at him as the tears slid down her cheeks. "You didn't have to stay, but you did, and you've given me the greatest gift. You let me meet Miley and get to know her." She returned her gaze to her parents. "I let Miley go once and, if I have a choice, I won't let her go again."

No one spoke for several moments. Zane's heart beat hard and he sat very still. Liv hadn't fought for him or Miley eleven years ago, but she was fighting for them now. Warmth and affection wrapped their way around his heart and he had to fight a surge of emotion rushing up his throat.

"I'm sorry everything happened this way," Zane finally said. "If you think it best, I can take the girls and leave. I can contact Liv away from the resort."

Liv's hand was still on Zane's arm and she squeezed it, ever so gently.

Marilyn looked at her hand, almost as if seeing it there for the first time, and then lifted her hard gaze to Zane. "Perhaps it's best—"

"No." Liv's voice was strong and sure. "Mom, Zane is a highly respected journalist. He came here to do a job and we shouldn't let anything prevent him from that. It could compromise his position with the magazine."

"Liv's right, Marilyn." Bob nodded. "Besides, Liv has met Miley. No matter what happens, she's an adult now and she can choose whether or not she wants to be a part of Miley's life." He looked at his wife. "It's not about us anymore. It's about Liv and Miley. We need to honor her wishes and do what she asks us to do. We owe her that."

Zane was torn. He didn't want Miley to feel unwelcome by Marilyn, yet he didn't want to take her away from Liv, either. He also needed this job and he wanted to write the article for Liv's sake, if not for her parents. She had done an amazing job on the resort and he was eager to showcase it in the magazine. With its rich history and family-run business model, it was exactly the kind of place he loved to write about.

But he wouldn't stay if it meant hurting Miley.

"What do you think?" Liv asked Zane, removing her hand from his arm at last. "Do you want to stay, given everything that's happened?"

Zane glanced between Liv's parents. Bob offered him a smile, but Marilyn refused to look him in the eyes.

"I guess it depends." Zane spoke carefully. "My biggest concern is for Miley."

"You don't need to be concerned," Bob said. "Marilyn and I will be just fine. Won't we?"

Marilyn looked at her husband and they studied one another for a heartbeat before she said, "Of course." She licked her lips and lifted her chin. "I'm just a little overwhelmed with the whole situation, but Bob's right. Olivia is an adult now and it's her choice to make. We tried to protect her as long as possible. It's not our place to interfere anymore."

"Then you'll be kind to Zane and his girls?" Liv asked.

"Of course I will, Olivia." Marilyn pursed her lips. "I'll treat them like any other guest who walks through our doors."

"What does Miley know?" Bob asked Zane.

"Nothing." He explained to them how he had met and married Tanya and how Miley believed Tanya was her biological mother.

"When will you tell her?" Marilyn asked.

"In our own time and way," Liv responded.

"Don't you think she should know as soon as possible?"

"No." Liv shook her head. "I want to wait until she gets to know me a little better. Zane already agreed to wait until we think she's ready."

"You mean," Marilyn said in a condescending voice, "when *you're* ready."

"When we're all ready," Zane corrected. "None of us saw this coming. We're trying to deal with it the best way we know how."

"And we'll honor that," Bob said. "Won't we, Marilyn?"

Marilyn sighed. "I guess we don't have any choice."

It wasn't really an answer, but it was probably the best they'd get out of Marilyn Butler.

"I should get back to the girls." Zane stood and Liv followed.

"Supper will be ready at six o'clock," Marilyn said. "We'll eat in the dining hall."

Bob rose with them. "Have you been out ice skating, yet?"

"Yesterday," Liv told him.

"What about sledding or snowshoeing? We have some cross-country skis, or you could try your hand at ice fishing."

"I promised the girls we'd take them sledding," Liv said.

"Good." Bob nodded. "I filled up about a dozen inner tubes before I left for the Twin Cities. They're in the winter shed."

Liv placed a kiss on his cheek. "Thanks, Dad."

He winked at her. "You're welcome, kiddo."

Liv and Zane left her parents' quarters and stood in the main room after Bob closed their door. The fire still crackled and a light snow had begun to fall outside the windows.

"Well," Liv said, shrugging, "I hope the worst is behind us."

"So do I." Zane tried to smile, but he couldn't shake the fear that their troubles had just begun.

Her brothers hadn't shown up yet.

Chapter Six

The sledding hill sat at the back of the resort, with an incredible view of Lake Madeline and the surrounding countryside. A thick blanket of snow covered the hill, which made riding down on their inner tubes a lot of fun. But climbing back up was a lot of work. Liv was out of breath from laughing and climbing with Zane and the girls. It felt good to get out of the lodge and breathe some fresh air—away from her mom.

Zane and Liv had purposely left the conversation back in the lodge so the girls' fun wouldn't be hampered. There wasn't a lot to say that hadn't already been said, so Liv forced herself to get lost in the moment. She loved watching Miley and Alexis speed down the hill, and she especially loved hearing their laughter. She had always wanted a sister, and the closest she'd ever come was her best friend, Piper. To see two sisters in action made her heart glad for both of them.

Thinking of Piper made Liv wonder what her friend would think when she learned about Miley. It would definitely come as a surprise, and there might even be some hurt feelings on Piper's part, but Liv was certain they could work things out. They'd been through a lot together in the past.

"My toes are getting cold," Zane said to Liv as he readjusted his stocking cap. His nose was red and fog billowed out of his mouth. "It's amazing how the girls don't seem affected by the weather."

It was true. They were trudging back up the hill, their black inner tubes in tow, as they chatted incessantly.

When they reached the top of the hill, Liv was about to tell the girls that this would be their last trip down when she saw two minivans pull into the resort parking lot.

Her brothers had arrived.

A groan escaped her lips before she could stop it.

Zane looked in the direction she was staring. "Ready for round two?" he asked Liv with a crooked smile.

The unease she felt at her brothers' arrival

soon melted away after seeing Zane's grin. She had faced off with her brothers several times before—defending her life choices, standing strong on her beliefs and convictions. But she had always stood alone. It felt comforting and freeing to know that this time she was standing with Zane beside her.

Five children piled out of the two minivans before Ben and Charlie and their wives exited. Charlie was the oldest. He and his wife, Rachel, had three children. Kendra, Leah, and Jackson. Ben was married to Megan and they had two children, Nicole and Anders. Liv loved being an aunt, and had looked forward to seeing her nieces and nephews over the Christmas break, but there were a lot of things she needed to deal with before she could fully enjoy their company.

Miley and Alexis stopped talking as they looked toward the parking lot.

"Who are they?" Alexis asked.

"Those are my brothers and their families," Liv said.

"Do they have any kids our age?" Miley asked.

"The oldest is nine and she's a girl named Kendra." Liv remembered holding little Kendra in her arms for the first time, only two years after giving up Miley. It had been one of the most heart-wrenching moments of her life. To know that Kendra was loved and wanted by her grandparents, but Liv's daughter had been despised and unwanted.

More than anything, Liv wanted her parents to accept Miley—then and now.

"There are two of them that are your age," Liv said to Alexis, squatting down to be eye-level with the five-year-old. They're both boys. Jackson and Anders."

Alexis scrunched up her nose at the word *boys*.

"Don't worry," Liv said to her, "they're the only boys, so they've learned how to play a lot of the games the girls love to play. And the girls aren't that much older than you. Leah and Nicole are seven. I think you'll like them." It had been hard to watch Megan and Rachel walk through their pregnancies together. They'd been pregnant at the same time with Leah and Nicole, and then Jackson and Anders. Though Liv was happy for them, she had still felt left out of their joy.

"They're staying here?" Miley asked.

"Yes. They'll be here until the day after New Year's, just like you."

"How about one more ride down the hill," Zane said, "and then we'll go and meet them."

The girls didn't give much of an opinion on

the idea, but Miley did look back at Zane and say, "How about this time, we all link hands as we go down?"

Zane glanced at Liv and she smiled at the idea.

"We'll go a lot faster, won't we?" Miley asked him.

He returned her smile and the four of them got onto their inner tubes. Liv and Zane were in the middle, holding hands, while Miley took Liv's mitted hand on one side and Alexis took Zane's on the other.

They sped down the hill, grasping hands. Liv almost lost Miley's grip as they twisted and turned, but she held on tight, laughing the whole way. It was impossible not to. Snow flew in their faces and Zane shared another smile with Liv as the girls squealed in glee.

When they finally arrived at the bottom of the hill, they picked up their inner tubes and started the trek back to the lodge.

Liv's nieces and nephews had run up to the lodge and were just being greeted by their grandparents when the sledding party arrived in the parking lot.

Mom and Dad hugged each grandchild, laughter and smiles on their lips as they asked them about their trip and told them all the fun and wonderful plans they had in store.

Liv's chest tightened at the scene and jealousy colored her vision thinking about the greeting Miley and Alexis had received, just a few hours earlier. There had been no laughter or joy in meeting Miley for the first time—only anger and disdain from her mom.

Ben and Charlie stood near each other, their arms crossed, as their wives spotted Liv and smiled at her arrival.

Megan, Ben's wife, had been the first to join their family and had always been one of Liv's favorite people. Megan and Ben had been high school sweethearts and had married the summer after graduation, much to Mom and Dad's dismay. But they were a happy couple and Megan was sweet and bubbly. She tempered Ben's gruff nature and was a fun addition to the family. Her short stature was in stark contrast to Ben's height, but neither one of them seemed to notice or care.

"Liv!" Megan left her husband's side and threw her arms around Liv. She squeezed her tight, whispering in her ear, "I've been praying for you ever since I heard."

Liv hugged her back.

"Hi, Zane," Megan said, her infectious smile brightening her pretty face. "It's so nice to see you again. And is this Miley and Alexis?"

"Hi, Megan." Zane nodded. "This is Miley," he put his mittened hand on her head, and then he scooped Alexis up into his arms, "and this is Alexis."

"Hi, girls," Megan said. She looked at Zane, her eyes shining with unshed tears. "They're beautiful."

Tears came easily to Megan, whether in happiness or sadness. She looked at Liv and smiled through the tears, then she pulled Liv into her embrace again and whispered, "I'm so happy for you." Then she glanced at the girls. "My children are close in age to you. Nicole and Anders are already at the lodge. They'll love meeting you."

Rachel, Charlie's wife, wasn't much of a hugger, but she did smile at Liv. She was taller, about Liv's height, and didn't wear her emotions on her sleeve in quite the same way as Megan. But she and Liv got along well and she offered Liv an understanding nod.

But Ben and Charlie were not smiling. They were both tall and muscular. Ben wore a baseball cap and was built like a mule. He lived for hockey and had taken over their dad's coaching job a few years back.

Charlie was the tallest and had a slimmer build. He wore a beard and had a stocking cap on his head. Both he and Ben stared at Zane for an uncomfortable amount of time.

"Hi, Zane," Rachel said. She had gone to high school with all of them but hadn't started dating Charlie until he had graduated. She hadn't been a part of their family when Miley was born. "I'm Rachel. I don't know if you remember me, but we had precalculus together."

Zane nodded and extended his hand to her. "I do remember you. It's good to see you again."

Rachel shook his hand and then glanced at her husband, but Charlie made no move to greet Zane.

There was nothing left but for Liv to say something. "Guys, this is Miley," she said to her brothers. "Zane's oldest daughter."

Her brothers looked in Miley's direction, but she shied away and stepped behind her father. Liv didn't blame her. Ben and Charlie were good guys—kind of like big teddy bears when they wanted to be—but they could also be imposing.

"And this is Alexis," Zane said, still holding her in his arms.

"Girls," Megan said, extending her hand out to Miley, "would you like to meet the kids? I bet Grammy has some hot chocolate ready for everyone."

Miley looked up at Zane with a question in her eyes and he nodded. She grinned and then took Megan's hand, as if she'd known her all her life. Alexis also agreed to go along with Megan, and Liv wasn't surprised. Megan was a kindergarten teacher and had an incredible rapport with children.

"I'll join you," Rachel said, scooting away from Charlie's side.

When they were out of hearing range, Ben crossed his arms and stared at Zane. "Are you here to cause trouble?"

Zane frowned. "No."

"Do you plan to hurt Liv?" Charlie asked.

"Of course not." Zane's frown deepened.

"Good." Ben nodded. "If you do either of those things, Charlie and I will personally toss you into the lake."

Liv rolled her eyes. "How about we all act like adults?"

Charlie shrugged. "That's the plan, as long as Harris doesn't do anything silly."

"I have no intentions of doing anything thoughtless," Zane said. "I'm just here to do a job."

Ben and Charlie continued to stare at Zane,

but Liv knew that they were only trying to protect her.

"How about you let me worry about myself?" Liv asked her brothers. "And let's all go inside. I'm freezing."

Liv's brothers left her side and walked toward the lodge, but Liv reached out and grabbed Zane's arm.

"I'm sorry, in advance, for anything that happens this week. My brothers mean well."

Zane's smile was quick and a bit disarming. He was close to Liv and he leaned a little closer. "I think it's sweet they care that much about you. Kind of gives me a little bit of comfort, actually, knowing you have so many people who love you so well."

Liv hadn't expected his response, nor the way it made her insides feel all warm and wobbly.

And she wasn't sure what made her more uncomfortable about the coming week: her family's unpredictability or her own emotions.

The lodge had quickly become overcrowded to Zane, even though there were dozens of guest suites and lots of communal space for everyone to spread out. But having Liv's parents and brothers there had suddenly made him feel like he was in the way.

Miley and Alexis had immediately hit it off with the nieces and nephews. After hot chocolate, they had gone into Bob and Marilyn's private quarters where there were a plethora of games and activities to be played.

But Zane didn't feel quite so ready to bond with Liv's family as the girls did. There were way too many memories between them to try to pretend everything was okay right now.

"I have an idea," Liv said to Zane as they set the hot chocolate mugs in the dishwasher inside the private quarters. "My mom and sisters-in-law will be busy making supper and the girls are occupied with my nieces and nephews. How would you like to get out of here and see a little more of the resort?"

Had she read his mind, or was his discomfort that visible? It didn't matter, because at that moment, he could have gathered her up in his arms and kissed her in gratitude. "I'd love that."

"Good." She smiled and set the last mug in place. "Put on something warm and meet me on the front deck in twenty minutes. I'll let Megan and Rachel know we're leaving and they'll help keep an eye on the girls."

Twenty minutes later, Zane was outside and

ready to go. The sky had become overcast again and a light dusting of snow was falling from the clouds. He took a deep breath of cold air, loving how it made his lungs tingle. It was so invigorating being back home in Minnesota. Everything looked more beautiful and peaceful than he remembered from his childhood.

"Ready?" Liv asked as she stepped through the front door and joined him on the deck. She wore a thick white coat and a pair of black snow pants. A knitted hat and scarf covered all but her nose and eyes, and on her hands were wool mittens. She looked warm and adorable.

"More than ready. Lead the way."

"I have a surprise for you." She led him off the deck and around the lodge to a large garage, nestled amongst the tall pine trees in back.

"Will I like it?"

Liv laughed. "I'm pretty sure you will. If not, you'll have to pretend, okay?"

He chuckled. "I can't make any promises."

She opened the service door and pressed a button, which caused one of the large garage doors to open. And there, sitting just behind the door, were two snowmobiles.

"When was the last time you drove one of these?" she asked him with a grin.

Zane couldn't stop smiling. "It's been years." He had loved driving a snowmobile when he was younger. He and his dad had owned a couple of them and taken them on several trips in Northern Minnesota. Some of his best memories with his dad were on those trips. "Are we going to take them out?"

"I'm hoping to take you on a tour of the property," she said. "Dad has made some really great trails and they wind all over the resort. But there's something buried deep in the woods I want to show you. I think it sets this place apart more than anything else."

Now she had him really intrigued. "Should I have brought my camera?"

"If you think you need pictures, I can bring you back."

They found some helmets and then got onto the machines. Both of them were fairly new and started up on the first try. The purr of the engine, the rumble of his seat and the smell of exhaust brought back dozens of memories.

He followed Liv out of the garage and into the deep, powdery snow. For ten minutes, they followed the trail leading away from the lodge, through the tall pine trees and up the hillside. If it hadn't been for the sound of the snowmobiles, it would have been so peaceful and calm. Even with the sound in his ears, the rush of being on the machine, combined with the beauty of nature around him, felt like he had pressed a reset button on the tension coiled in his gut.

Liv stayed ahead of him, pushing her machine to speeds that surprised him. He grinned when she revved her engine and turned to smile at him.

They climbed steadily, but gradually, uphill. Once in a while, he had a peek at the lake through the trees. Though it was frozen over, it was still a majestic site to behold.

He was wondering where she was bringing him when she led him into a clearing and came to a stop.

Zane's eyes opened wide at the incredible view before him.

They were at the top of the hill, with trees all around, but the clearing allowed them to have the best panoramic view of the lake. It spread out to the left and right, and as far as his eye could see to the horizon, where the sun was just starting to set. Lake Madeline was one of the largest lakes in the state and was home to some of the finest houses. He could see some of them now, standing proudly on the shoreline.

But it was the tree house, built around the top of an oak in the middle of the clearing, that made his mouth open wide. He had never seen anything like it. It wasn't just a tree house. It looked like a little cabin, built at least twenty feet in the air.

Liv pulled off her helmet and watched Zane's reaction. She turned off her snowmobile and smiled at him.

He switched off his machine and took off his helmet, too.

"What do you think?" she asked.

"What is this place?"

"It's called Hilltop." She got off her snowmobile and tilted her head toward the structure. "Want to see it?"

Zane nodded. He got off his machine and put his helmet on one of the handles.

A set of steps twisted around the base of the tree to the front door. They climbed up, and Liv unlocked the door.

The tree house was huge. It was chilly, since the heat wasn't on, but it had a small kitchenette, a large bed, a sitting area and a door, which he assumed went into a bathroom. The trunk of the oak ran right up through the middle of the room. But it was the windows, which encircled the tree house, that made his breath pause. They had a perfect three-hundred-and-sixty-degree view from the top of the tree. If he thought the lake looked majestic from below, up here it looked almost unearthly.

"Hilltop is available for rent," Liv said to Zane as she walked to one of the windows. "It's already booked every weekend from Memorial Day to Labor Day."

"This is incredible." Zane looked around the space, taking in the little details. "I've never seen anything quite like it. I'll definitely need to bring back my camera. This, alone, deserves an article for *Minnesota Moments Magazine.*"

"My dad hopes to build a few more along the hillside, but I don't think any of them will be quite as magnificent as this one." She leaned against the windowsill and watched Zane. "I took the long way to get here, but there's a much more direct path from the main lodge. Guests will be able to drive right up to the base of the tree."

Zane shook his head in wonder. "This place is amazing, Liv. Did you design it?"

A gentle smile tilted her lips and she nodded.

"You're a talented designer. I'm really impressed."

"Thank you. That means a lot to me."

"I'm serious." He walked over to where she stood. "I've been to a lot of places around the world and this has to be among my top five favorites. It's incredible. I'd love to stay here sometime. It would make a memorable place for a honeymoon—or a retreat," he added quickly.

Color tinged her cheeks and she looked away.

He needed to change the subject, afraid he had embarrassed her. "Thank you for bringing me here, and thank you for standing up for Miley with your family. I know this can't be easy for you."

She took a deep breath and the smile slipped from her face. "I should have done it a long time ago."

"It doesn't really matter now." He wanted her to look at him again, so he tilted his head to try to get into her line of sight. It worked. "All that matters is that you're doing it now."

Her eyes were so blue, especially here, with the daylight streaming in through the windows. How many times had he thought about her eyes over the years? Too many to count. A longing he hadn't felt for her in years began to grow inside him. They were truly alone for the first time and there were so many things he wanted to say.

She studied him, her quiet presence almost as unnerving as the noise back at the lodge. His mind suddenly felt muddled and his emotions mixed up.

He needed to focus on Miley right now and what all of this meant for his daughter—not what it meant for him.

"What do you think of Miley?" he finally asked her.

The most amazing look filled Liv's face, shining bright from her eyes. "There are no words to describe what I am thinking and feeling right now. She's incredible, Zane. Beautiful, silly, kind and rambunctious. She's everything and nothing I imagined. I'm blown away. Truly."

Her words filled his chest with warmth.

"And Alexis." She chuckled and her face softened even further. "She's adorable and quirky. They're both so amazing, I can't even begin to tell you how impressed I am with your parenting. The more I get to know them, the more I want to know them. Now I understand why God gives you a lifetime to get to know your children. It takes a lifetime to uncover all the little things that make them unique and wonderful."

"I couldn't say it any better." He leaned against the windowsill next to her. "They think you're pretty wonderful, too." He was close to Liv—really close—but he leaned closer, until their shoulders touched. "*I* think you're pretty amazing."

The color in her cheeks deepened, but she didn't look at him. "The feeling is mutual, Zane."

He had the urge to reach out and pull her into his arms but knew it was a foolish notion. They needed space and time to sort all of this, and didn't need anything to get in their way.

"We should probably head back," she said, moving away from the windowsill. "It's going to get dark soon."

Zane followed her out of the tree house and back to the snowmobiles. He was both relieved to be leaving the intimate space and sad that they were heading back to all the chaos.

Chapter Seven

Supper was noisy and chaotic that night. Thankfully, they were sitting in the large dining room, with the children at their own table, but it was still loud.

And Liv loved every second of it.

She glanced at the kids' table where Miley and Alexis were intermixed with the Butler cousins. They fit right in. If someone had come across this family gathering, they would never have suspected that the girls were newcomers. They laughed and talked with the others as if they'd known them their whole lives. Liv had barely seen them since she and Zane came back from Hilltop. The kids had been playing nonstop all afternoon.

But it was the grown-up table that held Liv's attention at the moment. Her mom and dad sat on opposite ends of the table, while

Ben and Megan sat near each other on one side and Charlie and Rachel sat side by side on the other. That left Liv sitting across from Zane. He caught her eye after she looked at the children and he smiled.

"I heard you've been living all over the world," Charlie said to Zane. "How'd you land a job like that?"

"It wasn't easy," Zane admitted. "I worked for a regional magazine right out of college and the owner had an editor friend who lived in London. They were looking for an American reporter and my boss recommended me for the job. My wife, Tanya, was exited to live there, so we packed up Miley and moved halfway around the world. While I was there, I started writing freelance travel articles for magazines back home. One thing led to another and I was traveling and living all over the world."

"That's incredible," Megan said. "I've always wanted to live outside the United States."

"You have?" Ben frowned as he looked at his wife.

"Wouldn't it be fun to live in Madrid or Paris?"

"And not know the language enough to ask for a bathroom?" The look of horror on Ben's face made everyone laugh.

"Seriously," Megan said as the laughter died down. "I'm a little envious of you and the girls."

"It wasn't always glamorous or easy," Zane conceded as Dad passed him a basket of bread. "I speak a little Spanish, but my French is abysmal, and I only know a couple of words in German. We've ended up in some pretty interesting situations for lack of communication skills."

As Zane told one story after the other, Liv watched her family listen. They were fully engaged and interested in his experiences. Even Mom, who had started the meal with a stiff back, was beginning to relax with Zane.

His stories were peppered with everyone's questions, and Zane came alive as he answered them. They laughed, cringed and Megan even cried, as Zane told them about people and places they had never seen before. Liv marveled that he could bring the stories alive in such an engaging and powerful way, and then she remembered he was a writer. It was his job to make them feel what he was feeling, see what he was seeing and hear what he was hearing.

It was remarkable.

"One of my favorite memories was catching an international hockey game between

Sweden and Finland." Zane cut into his chicken cacciatore and took a bite.

"You like hockey?" Charlie asked in surprise. "I thought your sport was basketball."

"I love hockey," Zane said with a shrug. "I just didn't get a chance to play it or watch it in high school because basketball was our family sport."

"Fair enough," Charlie said with a nod. "I can understand family loyalty."

Ben tilted his head toward the window and the lake beyond. "Maybe we'll get a chance to play a matchup while we're here."

"I'd like that." Zane nodded and caught Liv's eye. He gave her a quick wink, and she knew he was doing this to bring a bit of peace to their gathering.

"I might even toss on a pair of skates and join you," Dad said.

"Oh, Bob!" Mom's voice was high and animated with excitement. "Would you really? I haven't seen you play a real game in years."

"Only if you cheer me on," Dad said with a laugh and a smile in her direction.

The conversation shifted to hockey then, as it almost always did around the Butler table, but everyone was quick to include Zane in the plans for a family game.

Liv was quiet as she observed the people

around her. For the first time in her life, she wasn't the odd one out. With Zane across from her, she was not the only single person at the supper table. Of course, no one made her feel that way intentionally, but with Megan and Rachel sitting next to their husbands, Liv had always felt a bit adrift and lonely.

Not tonight.

Zane's glances made her feel noticed. When he purposely asked her questions, or tried to draw her into the conversation, she felt seen and appreciated. And she liked it. A lot.

Soon, the dishes were cleared and the playing cards were distributed. The lowest three numbers were given kitchen duty while the others went upstairs to the main room where a game of charades was being organized.

Liv and her parents had the three lowest cards, so they worked in the kitchen long after everyone had gone.

"I'm looking forward to that hockey game," Dad said as he put another stack of plates by the large, industrial dishwasher. The metal box sat on the top of the sink and washed large loads of dishes at record speed.

"I just hope you don't pull a muscle." Mom shook her head, but Liv could see she was happy that her dad intended to play again.

"Zane was a surprise," Dad said to Liv.

"How so?"

"He fit right into the family tonight."

"And that surprised you?"

Dad shrugged. "I guess so."

Liv stopped putting the glasses into the dish rack and looked at her dad. "Why?"

"I don't know." He leaned against the counter. "I just thought he wouldn't have anything in common with the rest of us."

"That's an odd assumption." Liv continued filling the dish rack, her thoughts on Zane, which wasn't unusual since his arrival. "He grew up in the same hometown as us and he and I had a lot in common in high school. We liked the same books, movies, music—"

"What are your intentions with him?" Mom interrupted Liv.

Not this again.

"I don't have any intentions, Mom." Liv pushed the dish rack into the washer and pulled down the top before pressing the button to run the machine. "We're taking things a day at a time."

Mom stood before the sink, scrubbing the baking dishes. She wore yellow rubber gloves and a white apron. The steam from the sink fogged up her glasses, but she didn't seem to mind. Mom had never minded kitchen work.

Liv suspected that she liked to take out her frustration on the dishes.

"You know what I mean," she said as she scrubbed furiously. "When the holidays are over. Are you hoping to be involved in their lives? Are you thinking about getting romantic again? Do you think Miley will accept you as her mother? Do you think Alexis will be jealous? How are you intending to handle all of it?"

Liv's head began to hurt. She stood by the machine, waiting for the light to turn off to indicate the wash cycle was complete. "I don't have any plans, Mom."

"You need to make plans, Olivia. But I don't think it would be smart to get romantically involved." Mom set the baking pan in the second sink to be rinsed. "Your first priority needs to be to Miley. It would only complicate things if you and Zane had to work through a romantic relationship, too."

"You don't need to worry about that. Zane and I have no plans to get romantically involved." Liv didn't think her mom had the right to ask these questions, but it was her mom. There was little she avoided when it came to her children's personal lives. "Besides, Zane has made no indication that he's even interested in me."

"I see the way he looks at you," Mom said, tackling the baking dish her husband handed her. "There's still a spark."

There was?

"Marilyn." Dad's voice held a warning tone. "Let her alone. She has enough to worry about with Miley. She doesn't need you poking at her love life, too."

"There's no love life to poke at," Liv protested.

"Leave it that way." Mom nodded once. "You two don't deserve a happily-ever-after with the way you messed things up."

Liv's mouth slipped open at her mom's harsh declaration and tears stung the backs of her eyes.

"Marilyn," Dad said again, but the wound had been inflicted already.

A memory floated to the surface of Liv's conscience—one she had suppressed from that long-ago day in the hospital when Miley was born. Her mom had been so angry, she had said a lot of things to hurt Liv. But it had been almost this very same sentiment that had hurt the worst. Her mother had told her she didn't deserve to be a mother. Moms were careful, selfless and wise. None of the things Liv had been when she got pregnant in high school.

And Liv had believed her—still believed her, if she was honest with herself.

She couldn't stay in the kitchen with her mom another moment. Tears threatened to spill down her cheeks as eleven years of pain accumulated in her heart and mind.

Liv left the kitchen, pulling the dish towel off her shoulder and tossing it onto the counter as she went. She didn't care if she was leaving her parents to finish up the work. Her mom's words burned deep, because she knew there was a bit of truth to them.

She and Zane had made a costly mistake—one that would eventually hurt Miley when she learned that she had been lied to—and abandoned—by her own mother. Liv couldn't be the cause of Miley's pain. She would be better off never knowing Liv was her mom.

The flames sparked and crackled in the fireplace as Miley and Kendra acted out a snowstorm while playing charades. The girls were giggling so hard they finally fell to the ground in fits of laughter after someone guessed it correctly.

Zane smiled at his daughter, thankful that she and Alexis had quickly bonded with the other children.

"Auntie Megan's team is next," Leah said, jumping up and down in excitement.

Bob and Marilyn had come upstairs about twenty minutes earlier and been absorbed into the two teams. Liv hadn't joined them, but Zane had assumed she went up to her suite for some reason. He looked toward the stairs, wondering where she might be. It seemed a little odd that she wouldn't be with the family.

So, where was she?

"Is Liv okay?" Zane asked as he leaned over to Bob. "Isn't she going to join us?"

Bob glanced at Marilyn, who pursed her lips and looked away.

Had something happened between Marilyn and Liv?

"She probably went outside to get some fresh air," Bob said.

In this cold?

Zane looked toward the large windows, but it was so dark outside, all he could see was blackness.

Jackson and Anders got up next and were acting out something Zane could not decipher. They were both so animated and serious, and their team was so determined to guess, everyone was shouting out ridiculous ideas.

But Zane couldn't stop thinking about Liv. Why did she need some fresh air? Had she fought with her parents? And, if so, had she fought about him and Miley? He hated to think she was suffering on his behalf. She shouldn't have to shoulder any of the burden alone.

"If I was going to look for her," Zane said to Bob, "where would I start?"

Bob's face softened with approval. "I'd start on the deck. I put a gas fire table out there. She might have lit it for some warmth. She usually goes outside when she needs to sort through her troubles."

Troubles? Zane glanced at Marilyn again, but she looked away from him.

"Thanks," Zane said to Bob. "I think I'll go see if she needs anything."

While everyone was busy trying to guess, Zane went up to his room and grabbed his jacket, hat and boots. He came back down the stairs and slipped out the front door with only Bob noticing. Zane nodded at Liv's dad and her dad smiled back.

Large, thick snowflakes fell from the inky black sky. Zane could not see far beyond the front deck of the lodge, but he didn't need to. Liv was sitting on one of the rocking chairs, near a gas fire table, just as her dad had predicted.

She was wearing her white coat, stocking cap and a large knitted scarf around her neck. A checkered blanket was on her lap, and her legs were pulled up so her knees were pressed against her chest. She had a steaming mug of something in her hands.

"Liv?"

Glancing up in surprise, she brushed at her cheek with her mitten before meeting his gaze.

"Mind if I join you?" he asked in a hushed voice, not wanting to disturb the stillness of the moment.

She shook her head but did not speak.

Zane took one of the other rockers away from the side of the lodge and moved it to the fire table. There was a layer of snow on it, but he brushed it off and took a seat. The heat from the flames cast just enough warmth to take the chill out of the air around the fire.

And it offered a beautiful glow, making Liv's eyes shine—though from the flames or the tears, he couldn't tell.

They both sat in silence for a long time as they looked into the fire. It felt good to have some time and space to just think about the last few days and all of the changes that had occurred in both their lives. And it felt good to sit in the quiet stillness with Liv, though he longed to know what had happened to bring her out here alone, with tears in her eyes.

"I'm sorry if my presence here is causing trouble between you and your family." He watched her, hoping she would reassure him that it wasn't a problem, but he knew it was.

"The trouble between me and my mom goes way back." She bit her bottom lip as she continued to look into the flames.

"Is this just about Miley, or is it deeper?"

She lifted a shoulder. "I suppose I struggled to meet my mom's expectations all my life, but it all came to a head when I got pregnant. Since then, I really haven't spent a lot of time with her, until she and Dad bought this resort and I started to help them renovate. I had thought our relationship was on the mend."

"Things were getting better before this week?"

"Ironically, yes. It felt like we had put it behind us." She shook her head and finally met his gaze. "But it was always there. We would have eventually needed to deal with it if we wanted to move forward. I'm just sad that you and Miley have to be here to see it."

"You don't need to worry about us, Liv.

You've got enough on your plate without adding our feelings to the mix."

"I appreciate that."

He was quiet again as he studied her. The firelight danced off the beautiful lines of her face. He was afraid to voice his next thoughts and hoped she wouldn't get angry at him. "I don't think the heaviness on your heart is just about your mom."

It was her turn to study his face, but she didn't look mad or upset at him.

"I don't think you've ever forgiven yourself for letting go of Miley."

She closed her eyes and put her head down on her knees. After a few moments, her shoulders began to shake with the tears he knew she was shedding.

Zane's heart broke for her and he left his seat. He took her mug and set it on the edge of the fire table, then he grasped her hands in his and pulled her to her feet, so he could wrap her in a tight embrace.

"It's okay, Liv," he whispered into her ear, running his hand up and down her back. "You don't need to blame yourself anymore. Miley has never, ever been hurt by you."

"But she will be, if she ever learns the truth."

"Maybe," he agreed, his voice soft and low,

"but ultimately, she'll forgive us and be a better person because of the truth. We have no idea how God will use this to strengthen her character."

"Forgive *us*?" She pulled back and looked up at Zane, tears on her cheeks. "Why would she need to forgive you? You didn't abandon her when she needed you most."

He stared at her, shocked that she took the full blame for what had happened. "Liv, both of us are responsible for Miley's life. I was going to give her up, too, if you remember. But circumstances changed."

"You made the biggest sacrifice of all and raised her."

"I didn't always make the sacrifice with a happy heart. I was angry and bitter a lot in those early years. When my peers were living happy, carefree lives our first few years of college, I was going home after a long day of school and several hours of work to take care of a baby. At the time, I wasn't happy about my circumstances."

She looked at him, her face a mask of emotions he couldn't begin to read.

"I have incredible guilt about those years," he continued. "I was probably more detrimental to Miley than you could ever be. I was impatient, grumpy and often short-tempered with her." He hated to admit this truth to Liv, but it needed to be done. She couldn't live under the false impression that he had been perfect as he raised their daughter. "If anyone needs to ask for her forgiveness, it's me."

"But all of that is in the past."

"And so is our mistake. But it led to the most precious gift of our lives—Miley. And, with God's help and Miley's love, you and I will be able to help our daughter deal with this difficult truth."

She put her arms around him again and pulled him into a tight hug.

His heart pounded at being this close to Liv again and he marveled at how well she fit into his embrace. Her hair smelled like flowers and she was soft under his hands.

"Thank you," she whispered.

He held her closer.

Finally, she pulled out of his arms, tears still wetting her cheeks. "Thank you for being there for our daughter when I couldn't be."

"You're welcome, Liv."

She slowly picked up her blanket and mug and then indicated the lodge. "I suppose we should rejoin everyone. I can't hide out here forever."

Zane nodded, though he wished they could have a few more minutes alone.

As they walked into the lodge, he realized she hadn't told him what had happened between her and her mom. Maybe it was best that he didn't know. He was struggling to hold his peace where Marilyn Butler was concerned, and the last thing Liv needed was for Zane to argue with her mom.

Chapter Eight

On Christmas Eve, Liv stood outside with her entire family and Zane and his girls, looking for the perfect Christmas tree. It had been two days since their fireside talk on the front deck, and since then, Liv had done her best to push aside the feelings of guilt she carried over Miley's birth. She wanted to believe Zane when he said he hadn't been a perfect father, though that didn't give her an excuse for what she had done to Miley. It did make her appreciate that Zane cared enough to shoulder some of the responsibility.

And, it had felt wonderful to be in his arms again, though she tried hard not to think about how her stomach had fluttered at his nearness or the way her insides had melted like warm wax. She would have stayed near the fire table with him longer, but she had been afraid of her feelings. She hadn't felt like that since high school, and she wasn't about to admit the truth to herself: he was undoing her resolve to remain uninterested in romance again.

"I like this one best," said Nicole as she pointed at one of the tallest evergreen trees in the woods.

"How would Grampy get that inside the lodge?" Miley asked, calling Liv's dad by the same name as all the other children did. At first, Liv was surprised, but then she realized it was only natural. She didn't even know if Miley and Alexis knew Grampy and Grammy's real names.

"He could cut off the roof of the lodge," Nicole said as she laughed hysterically at her own joke. The other kids thought it was hilarious, too, and joined in the silliness.

"I like this one," Rachel said, walking over to a more realistic tree.

"We found the perfect one," Ben called out from a short distance away. "Come over here."

Everyone hiked through the knee-deep snow to the tree that Ben, Charlie and Zane were standing around.

It was perfect.

"This should fit in the front room," Mom

said as she walked around the tree, looking at each side with a critical eye. "It's full, with good branches, and isn't too wide."

Everyone stood back, waiting for her final verdict, since it was her home and her tree.

"What does everyone else think?" she asked.

Liv wished she wouldn't have. Each of the kids had their own idea of the "perfect" tree and voiced those opinions now.

Thankfully, Megan got them all to quiet down. "This is Grammy's tree," she said. "Let's let her make the final decision."

"I think this one will do," Mom said with a nod. "I like it."

Dad had brought along an electric chain saw and he turned it on while Liv, Megan and Rachel shooed the kids away from the tree. Zane held the trunk at the top, while Ben and Charlie pulled branches away from the stem so Dad could get on his knees to cut it down.

"Timber," Dad called a couple seconds later, but it wasn't necessary, since Zane was holding the tree and it couldn't go anywhere.

The kids laughed and squealed in delight as Ben and Zane hefted the tree to their shoulders and they all started the trek back to the lodge.

"O, Christmas tree, o, Christmas tree, how

lovely are your branches," Megan began to sing as they followed the men. The kids were soon singing along. When that carol was finished, Megan began another and another until they were inside the lodge with the tree.

Dad had already set the tree stand in place in the corner of the main room, between the fireplace and one of the windows. While the men worked at getting it in place, Mom, Rachel and Liv went to get the boxes of ornaments and decorations from the storage room. Megan kept the kids occupied. They were making a paper snowflake garland in the private quarters. They had been working on it for the past two days.

Within the hour, the tree had been strung with white lights and it was time to put on the ornaments. Each Butler child had their own box, including the grandchildren and Rachel and Megan. Liv had twenty-eight ornaments, one from each year. Even after she had moved out, her mother had continued the tradition. No doubt, she would get another one this year.

"Each person is responsible for hanging their own ornaments," Liv said to Miley and Alexis as they came over to see inside her box. "But you can help." She smiled at the girls, who looked eager to hang a few ornaments. "Would you like to hang some of mine?"

"Yes!" both of the girls said at the same time.

"This one is the oldest," Liv said, pulling out a blown-glass teddy bear with a red Santa Claus hat on its head. "My parents gave this one to me when I was first born."

Miley's eyes opened wide. "It must be *really* old."

Zane's laughter filled the air right behind Liv and she turned to give him a teasing glare. "I don't think that's funny enough to warrant your laughter, Mr. Harris."

He pressed his lips together, but his shoulders still shook with mirth.

"Is this one old?" Alexis asked as she pulled out a ceramic ballerina, the paint aged and cracked with time.

"It is," Liv said. "My mother gave that one to me the year I started taking ballet lessons when I was three."

"I was three when I started taking lessons," Miley said.

"You're a dancer?" Mom asked as she came up behind Miley.

Miley nodded. "I love dancing." To prove her point, she did a pirouette.

Mom simply nodded and then left the room.

The girls helped Liv hang her ornaments as she told them about each one. It was crowded around the tree as everyone worked, and Zane stood off to the side, simply watching.

A few minutes later, Mom returned to the room with a bag full of small wrapped packages. "This year's ornaments," she said to everyone as she pulled one after the other out of the bag, reading off the names of each. Mom was good about finding an ornament that matched the personality or interests of each person.

As the kids were opening their ornaments, Liv looked down at Miley and Alexis, wishing she had something for them. "I'm sorry you don't have an ornament to open—"

"Don't speak so quickly," Mom said to Liv as she pulled three more boxes out of her bag. "I have a small collection of ornaments I keep hidden away. Sometimes, when I'm shopping, I pick them up, thinking I'll use them, but then I find one or two that work better." She handed a box to Miley and then to Alexis. "I think you might like these."

The girls' eyes shone and they tore off the wrapping paper.

"A ballerina!" Miley said as she pulled the delicate ornament from the box. It twirled on its string and Miley's shoulders came up in delight.

"A puppy!" Alexis said as she pulled hers out of the packaging. "I love puppies."

"And don't think I forgot about you, Zane," Mom said as she walked up to him.

"You didn't have to, Marilyn."

"Nonsense." She lifted her chin a little, something new in her eyes. "You're practically family, as Bob reminded me last night. You and the girls should have your own ornaments, since I don't think this is the only Christmas you will be celebrating with us in some way or other." She sent a meaningful look in Miley's direction.

Liv held her breath. Would Mom go too far and say something to Miley?

Thankfully, she stepped back and closed her mouth, waiting for Zane to open his ornament.

When he did, he pulled out a small globe. It was beautiful and intricate, the countries created out of a mosaic of colors, with all of them outlined in gold. "It's beautiful," Zane said to Mom. "Thank you."

"It's a reminder," Dad said, coming up behind Mom, putting his hands on her shoulders. "You may wander the earth but know that you always have a home here at Lakepoint Lodge."

"I appreciate that." Zane nodded, clearly moved by what Dad had said. "Thank you."

Zane walked over to the tree, where Liv was still standing. "Is this okay?" he asked her, indicating the ornament and the tree.

She nodded. "You and the girls are family," she said, for just their ears alone. "I hope we have many more happy Christmases together."

"So do I." He smiled at her and then placed his ornament on the tree, near Miley's and Alexis's ornaments.

And Liv hoped, with all her heart, that their family was starting to heal.

The tree was soon finished and the rest of the Christmas decorations were being displayed around the lodge. Zane helped Ben hang pine garland on the stairway railing, along the thick beams over the front desk and on the fireplace mantel. While they worked, he and Ben visited, and he realized they had a lot more in common than Zane first thought. It almost felt like he was meeting Ben Butler for the first time. All of his preconceived ideas about Ben and Charlie had been slowly evaporating the past two days. They were hardworking dads who cared about their families and their work, just like Zane.

It made him wonder how many other people he had misread in high school.

Liv kept Miley and Alexis busy with putting out the Nativity display, weaving red ribbon through the garland and hanging old family bells that had been handed down through the generations of Butlers.

Every once in a while, Zane caught Liv telling the girls about a family tradition or a special decoration, and he couldn't help but wonder what Liv was thinking and feeling. She had waited eleven long years to share these things with her daughter and probably never thought she'd get the chance. He couldn't help but thank God that their reunion had been orchestrated, without their foreknowledge.

"Who is ready for some quiet time?" Megan asked as she stacked an empty rubber tote in the corner.

The kids all groaned, but Megan's smile only grew brighter. "Grammy and Grampy have some popcorn and cookies waiting in their kitchen, and I have *How the Grinch Stole Christmas* queued up on their television."

Everyone's groans turned to cheers, and the

kids soon disappeared from the main room and the door to Grammy and Grampy's private quarters closed.

"I could go for a nap," Ben said as he scratched behind his ears in a habit he'd had since he was young.

"Same." Charlie yawned. "Rachel already went up to our suite to read for a while."

"I think we're done down here," Liv said to her brothers. "And the kids will be occupied for a while. Go take a nap."

Liv's brothers didn't protest, and soon the main room was empty of everyone but Liv and Zane.

"What about you?" Liv asked as she picked up a random scrap of paper on the floor and tossed it into a recycling bin. "Are you tired?"

Zane shook his head. "I usually feel energized after a lot of chaos. I can't rest until I run or do something physical to work out the tension."

Liv's smile was quick and a bit surprised. "Me, too." She nodded toward the outside. "Want to go cross-country skiing or snowshoeing with me?" She added quickly, "Unless you'd rather be by yourself. No one's had a quiet moment since everyone arrived."

"Actually," Zane said, "I'd rather not go by myself." The truth was, he wanted to be alone with Liv. He hadn't had a moment of quiet with her since their talk on the deck a couple days ago, and as strange as it was to admit, he missed her, even though they'd been together almost nonstop in the presence of everyone else.

"Okay." Liv's smile was sweet and suddenly shy. "Let's meet back here in about ten minutes. I'll let Megan and my mom know where we're going and they can watch the girls."

"Sounds like a good plan." Zane left the main room and went up to change into some outdoor clothes. Since he would be working hard, he didn't put on his snow pants and thick jacket. Instead, he opted to wear his cold-weather running clothes, which would offer some protection against the elements but wouldn't cause him to overheat.

When he rejoined Liv, he found that she'd had the same idea. She wore a lightweight jacket and a pair of thick black yoga pants with a scarf, hat and gloves.

She was in great shape and the muscles in her calves and thighs were well-defined. It was clear she was still very active. He loved that she enjoyed the outdoors as much as he did.

"Do you still run like you used to?" Zane

asked, recalling how well she had done in cross-country running and track and field in high school. She had broken some of the school records.

"I do."

"I wasn't much of a runner before we dated," he said as they walked out the front door, remembering how much she had bugged him to run with her. When he finally agreed to start, he had never stopped. It had become a life-long activity. "I've run in some pretty amazing places all over the world."

"I can almost imagine it," she said with a smile in her voice.

They walked across the deck and down the steps.

"In a way," he said quietly, "you were there with me."

She hesitated a moment and then continued to lead him on the path to the large garage behind the lodge. She glanced at him. "How was I there with you?"

"Every time I put on my running shoes, I thought of you and how you had pestered me to start running." He chuckled. "I can't even begin to tell you how important those runs became to me over the years. And each time I was thankful I had started to run, I was thankful you had been the one to encourage me to start."

Liv finally paused, the snow-laden pine trees a beautiful backdrop behind her. "Why were your runs so important?"

Zane hadn't talked much about Tanya since his arrival, and Liv hadn't asked. He hadn't been sure how much to tell her, but there was no reason not to be honest. If he and Liv were going to work together to raise Miley—which was what he hoped she wanted—then she had a right to know more about the woman who had been Miley's only mother for eight years of her life.

"At first, they were just for exercise or to blow off stress from work," he said, starting to walk toward the garage again. "Then, I started to run after Tanya and I argued. I found myself running more and more, just to work out the anger and tension from our fights."

"I'm sorry," Liv said gently. She didn't unlock the service entrance but went to the back of the garage and opened a door that led into a lean-to shed. All the gear they would need to go cross-country skiing was inside.

"I haven't talked with you much about Tanya," Zane said as he looked over the skis and shoes and found ones he thought might work for him. "We tried not to fight around the girls, so the memories of their last few months with her are pretty happy. I try not to say anything negative about her around them."

"I completely understand. They've told me a lot about Tanya and I know they both loved her very much."

Zane nodded. "Tanya was a great mom. She loved taking the girls sightseeing wherever we lived and she was so good at making every experience unique and memorable for them. She enjoyed cooking and took lessons from chefs in almost every city we lived in. Her laughter was so infectious, sometimes we just laughed because she was laughing." He paused as he took a seat on the bench lining the shed wall. How could he summarize Tanya's amazing personality in only a few sentences?

Liv sat next to him and they exchanged their winter boots for the ski shoes.

"What went wrong?" Liv asked.

He almost didn't want to admit the truth. It still stung every time he thought about it, even now, several years later. He stuck his foot into the ski shoe and pulled the straps tight.

"It was complicated and I was just as much

to blame as Tanya." The shoe fit perfectly, so he zipped up the outer cover and moved on to the next one. "I knew she was unhappy for a while, but I was so preoccupied with my work, I didn't pay much attention. She had always enjoyed traveling, but the last few months before she died, she was ready to come back to the States and settle down. I wasn't. She wanted to leave Rome soon after we arrived, but I had just landed the job and I didn't want to quit. I felt justified in my actions, because it was my job and I was providing for my family. I didn't feel it was fair for her to put pressure on me to give up everything I had worked so hard to achieve."

"So, you began to fight."

The air was so still and calm around them. Bright sunshine filled the world with a dazzling brilliance. It felt like he was a million miles away from all those fights in Rome. Yet they had ultimately dictated this very moment. "The fights seemed inconsequential at first. She wanted to leave, but I wasn't ready. But then, one day, after the worst fight we'd ever had, I came home from a run and found a neighbor lady babysitting the kids. Tanya had left and didn't tell me where she was going. She didn't answer her phone for hours. When she finally came home, she refused to tell me where she had been."

Liv sat up straighter to listen to Zane's story. Her blue eyes were filled with concern and the faintest frown lines slanted across her forehead.

Zane finished zipping up his shoes, and though he was looking at Liv, his thoughts were fully captivated by Tanya and those last few months. "She disappeared more and more often. I worked at home, mostly, and at first, she would tell me she was running to the market, but it would take her hours longer than usual. Then, she would simply tell me she was going out and not say where or when she was coming home. When I started to demand that she tell me, we would only fight more."

Liv didn't say a word as she listened, and Zane realized he didn't need her to say anything. It was nice just to talk about this part of his life. His parents knew a little, but even then, he didn't want their memories of Tanya to be tainted by what had happened. Since they had moved around so much, Zane didn't have any close friends to rely upon. Telling Liv all of this now felt good, but he didn't want to color Liv's opinions about Tanya, either.

"What happened?" Liv asked.

"I want you to know the truth," he said to her, "but I don't want you to think Tanya was a bad mom. She made some poor choices in the end, but—"

"Zane," Liv said gently, "I, of all people, understand the need for grace and forgiveness. It's taken me a long time—and, to be honest, I'm not quite there yet—but I'm starting to realize that our mistakes don't have to define who we are. Everyone has things in their past that they aren't proud of. But our poor choices don't make us inherently bad people."

"Thanks, Liv." He loved that she was offering grace to Tanya, even before she knew what had happened.

"How could I not think highly of her?" Liv asked. "Miley and Alexis are amazing little girls. They are so courteous and thoughtful. My opinion of Tanya is already very high." The same shyness from before tinged her cheeks and she looked down at her hands. "And, if you chose her to be your wife, she must have been very special."

His heart warmed at her words. He was thankful his past, and his memories of Tanya, were safe with her. "The day I learned Tanya had died in a cab accident in Rome, I also learned that a man had died with her. His name was Antonio Rossi. She had been seeing him for several months. After her funeral, I found dozens of text messages and emails they had exchanged. He had been begging her to leave me and stay in Rome with him, but she had told him many times that she didn't want to break up our family or take the girls from me. Another set of emails I found were between Tanya and her sister, and she had told her sister that she was begging me to take her back to the States because she didn't think she could resist Antonio's attraction for much longer." Zane looked away from Liv and leaned forward to put his elbows on his knees. "I don't know when she met Antonio, or how far she had taken the relationship, but looking back at her increased anxiety and our fights, I think it was going on for quite a while and it had become very serious." His heart was heavy, as always, when he thought about those last few months. "If I had not been so selfish, all of it would have been different. Tanya would probably still be alive and the girls would have their mom."

"Zane." Liv put her gloved hand on his shoulder. "It's not your fault. It was an accident. No one could have predicted it."

"But if I had agreed to come back to the States, she wouldn't have been in that cab."

"How were you supposed to know? You were pursuing a career and income to support your family. Thousands of married couples fight about that very thing. You thought you were doing the best thing for your family."

"But Tanya was so unhappy with our lifestyle and wanted to leave."

"From what you've told me, she loved traveling and exploring new places. I don't think her unhappiness was in your lifestyle, but in her own attraction to a man she wasn't married to." Liv ran her hand over Zane's back. "It sounds like she became desperate to return to the States so she could physically remove herself from the temptation of Antonio, and not because she was dissatisfied with the life you were providing."

Zane knew it was true, yet the guilt he had carried over Tanya's death was still heavy.

"Just because her circumstances changed doesn't mean it was your fault," Liv continued. "Her unhappiness in staying in Rome sounds like it had more to do with Antonio than with you."

Perhaps Liv was right. Maybe Tanya's desire to come home had been *because* of Antonio. It didn't relieve the responsibility he still felt, but it did release some of the burden he had carried for her unhappiness.

He straightened and met Liv's gaze. "Thank you."

"For what?"

"For letting me talk and for helping me to unravel some of the past."

"Sometimes we're too close to a situation to see it clearly and we need another person's perspective." Her eyes were soft as she studied him. "That's what you've offered to me, Zane, with Miley's birth. You've helped me to see it from your eyes and you offered me a lot of grace and forgiveness. I hope I can do the same for you."

She was so close and so lovely, his heart pounded hard from the feelings she stirred within him. She possessed all the qualities he had loved about her in high school, yet she had grown and matured into an even more stunning and wonderful person.

"Miley was blessed to have Tanya as her mom." Zane's voice was thick with emotion. "And she's blessed to have you, too."

Liv's eyes filled with tears and she looked away, embarrassed. "I haven't cried in years, and look at me now!" She laughed as she wiped the tears away. "It still feels a bit surreal to hear you talk about me as her mom."

"I hope that someday, very soon, she learns

the truth, and she's just as pleased with saying it as I am."

Things were getting much too serious, so he stood and offered her his hand. "Are you ready? I can't wait to see more of the resort."

Liv wiped the last of her tears and nodded.

He was looking forward to spending a quiet hour with her, skiing through the woods, before taking her back to the lodge to share her again.

Chapter Nine

"Liv! Wake up! The presents are here!" Miley's excited voice filtered through the door of Liv's suite.

"I'm awake!" Liv called back as she opened the door, a smile on her face. "Merry Christmas."

Miley stood in her pajamas with Alexis by her side. Alexis was wearing a princess dress and a tiara. It was still dark outside, but inside, the children were making a ruckus awakening their parents and grandparents.

"Merry Christmas!" Miley said. "Can we have our presents now?"

A door opened down the hallway and Zane appeared. He was wearing pajama bottoms and a T-shirt, his hair mussed from sleep. He also wore his black-framed glasses and appeared far too handsome for that early in the morning. "Girls," he whispered loudly. "It's six o'clock. Let Liv sleep."

"It's okay." Liv smiled, trying not to stare at him. He was so good-looking it was almost impossible not to stare. "I heard my nieces and nephews running through the hallway, so I was already awake." She had on a robe and her hair was in a messy bun, but she'd managed to wash her face and brush her teeth before Miley and Alexis arrived.

"Well," he said, rubbing his eyes under his glasses, "we're up. We might as well stay up."

"Yay!" Miley and Alexis cheered.

"I'll make some coffee," Liv told Zane, "and meet you by the tree in a couple of minutes."

"It's a date." He smiled at her and her stomach fluttered.

She closed her door and leaned against it for a heartbeat. She knew he'd been teasing about the date, but it was getting harder and harder to deny the attraction she felt for him. Even if she forced herself not to notice or pay attention to the feelings, they still took her by surprise, at the oddest moments.

There was no time to get dressed fully for the day, but she wanted some coffee. The small kitchenette in her room was equipped with everything she needed, so she brewed a pot while she brushed her hair and changed out of her pajamas into some comfortable clothes.

When she stepped out of her room, Zane was just leaving his. They smiled at each other and she passed him his cup of coffee. He had changed, but he hadn't taken the time to shave. A shadow of a beard lined his cheeks and chin and made him look even more handsome.

"The girls already went down," he said as he paused and took a sip of the coffee. "I couldn't rein them in for another second."

"I'm sure my mom is there holding them back from their gifts until the adults come down."

"I hope your mom is okay that I added my gifts for the girls among the others around the tree."

"Of course she is." Liv couldn't imagine her mother having a problem with a few extra gifts.

They walked down the grand staircase and into the main room. Dad had already started a fire in the fireplace and the lights were lit on the tree. All seven of the kids were licking candy canes and sitting on the floor in their pajamas, while all the parents were dozing on the furniture.

"It's nice that you could finally join us," Charlie teased when he saw Liv and Zane.

"I needed some coffee," Liv said as she shrugged.

Dad and Mom entered the room with a tray of cups and two steaming pots. "One has hot chocolate and the other has coffee," Mom said with a big smile. "Merry Christmas, everyone."

There was a chorus of Merry Christmases while Liv took a seat on one of the sofas.

Zane sat next to her.

She tried not to notice his nearness, but he was sitting so close, their legs brushed together.

Dozens and dozens of wrapped gifts peeked out from under the beautiful tree. The noise level was at an all-time high as the children begged their parents to start opening.

"This will take a while," Liv warned Zane as she whispered into his ear. "My mom likes to see each person open their gifts, so we do this one at a time."

Zane lifted his eyebrows and nodded, a smile on his face. "Then I'm happy I have my coffee."

"Don't worry, my mom will let us break for some food in about an hour." Liv giggled, her heart light and cheerful. She still couldn't believe she was celebrating Christmas morning with her daughter—and Zane.

He smiled at her and she smiled back, loving how she felt so close to him, in both body and purpose. They were working together for the good of Miley. It had created a bond unlike any she'd ever experienced before.

Mom and Dad sat closest to the tree, handing out each package. They tried to make everything even, so that each person could open one gift per round. When all the gifts were opened and admired, Mom and Dad handed out another round and they did it again.

Thankfully, Zane had brought several gifts for the girls, and Mom had a few things in reserve that she was able to give to them. Liv didn't have much and there wasn't a store close enough for her to shop, so she had relied on her sisters-in-law, who had rearranged a few things and gave a couple presents to Liv that she was able to give the girls.

"Next Christmas," Liv said quietly to Zane as she watched Miley open up one of the gifts she had given to her daughter, "I will be fully prepared and will have lots of gifts ready for the girls."

"It's okay," he said. "You didn't know. Besides, they are having the time of their lives this week. They will soon forget the packages they opened, but they'll never forget the fun they had with you."

"Do you always know what to say?" she asked with a smile as she nudged his shoulder.

"I *am* a writer," he said with a playful shrug.

Miley's face lit up with joy when she discovered a popular series of books inside her package.

"Do you have them?" Liv asked.

"No!" Miley jumped up and came to Liv. "Thank you for the books. I'm going to *love* them!" She lunged into Liv's arms to hug her. "Thank you, thank you, thank you, Liv."

Liv held her daughter, tears springing to her eyes without warning. "You're welcome, Miley."

All the adults were watching the two of them and Megan even wiped away a stray tear. Liv loved that her family had been so warm and welcoming to Zane and the girls this week. Even her mom had been kind after the initial shock.

What had Liv been so worried about?

As Miley left her and went back to show off the books to the other girls, Liv's heart began to beat hard and her stomach filled with nerves. Maybe today would be the day to finally tell Miley the truth. It was Christmas, after all, and what better day would there be? There was little reason to put it off anymore. Liv was no longer a stranger to Miley and she seemed to like her. Why should she wait?

"I think I'm ready," Liv said quietly to Zane.

He looked at her, understanding dawning in his gaze. "Now?"

"No." She shook her head quickly. "Later, when we can be alone with her—that is, if you're okay with telling her."

"I am." He smiled and his whole face lit up with joy.

Her hands were shaking so hard, she squeezed them together.

Zane reached over and put his hand over them. "It will be okay, Liv. I promise."

His calm voice and steady presence were enough to lower her heart rate, but her stomach still turned with nerves.

"Anyone ready to eat?" Mom asked.

Several people called out their approval and Mom left the room. A few minutes later, she came back with a tray of pastries and a wrapped box. "I forgot this gift in my room."

"Who is it for?" Kendra asked, her eyes wide with hope.

"Just a minute," Mom said with a smile. She handed the tray off to Ben who took a napkin and a pastry and then passed it on to Megan. As the tray moved around the room, Liv didn't take anything to eat, her stomach in knots. She wouldn't be able to even think about food until they had a chance to talk to Miley.

Mom took a seat near the tree again and she and Dad passed out another round of gifts. The one she had brought in from her room was handed to Miley.

"For this round, I want Miley to open first," Mom said.

Liv frowned, curious what her mom had in the box. Miley and Alexis had already opened the few presents Liv knew about. What could this one be?

"Okay," Miley said with a grin. She got up on her knees and tore the wrapping paper off as everyone watched.

"Be very careful," Mom warned. "It's old and delicate."

Old and delicate? Why would her mom give Miley something so old she had to warn her to be careful?

"What is it?" Liv asked her mom.

"You'll see," she said with a secretive smile.

Miley finally opened the box and she inhaled a deep breath. "It's beautiful!"

"What is it?" Megan asked, peering over Nicole's head for a peek.

"It's a ballet tutu," Miley said as she pulled it from the box. It was lemon yellow, with golden sparkles, and looked very familiar.

Liv's heart sank at the sight of it and she looked at her mom with a question forming on her lips.

"I thought she should have something of her mother's," Mom said with a shrug. "And since she loves ballet, why not let her have one of her mother's costumes?"

"This was my mom's?" Miley asked, her eyes wide as she hugged the tutu to her body. "I didn't know my mom was a dancer! I love it!"

A lump formed in Liv's throat as she watched Miley cradle the tutu tenderly, believing it had belonged to Tanya. What would she think when she learned the truth?

"She was a dancer," Mom said, "and I know she would love to dance with you someday."

It was Miley's turn to frown.

Zane stood, his face white.

Liv felt like she was going to be sick.

"How can my mom dance with me?" Miley asked, pain and confusion on her brow. "My mom died."

The kids got very quiet and the adults didn't move.

"She's not dead," Mom said. "She's right here."

"Mom," Liv said, shaking her head. "Don't."

"My mom is here?" Miley's eyes filled with tears as she looked at her dad. "What does she mean, Daddy?"

"This isn't funny, Marilyn," Zane said. "You had no right."

"What were you thinking?" Liv asked her mom.

"I was thinking this child needs to know the truth." Mom stood and put her hands on her hips. "I'm tired of everyone lying to her. It's cruel not to tell her."

Miley ran to her father and buried her face into his stomach.

"Stop it," Dad said to Mom. "You shouldn't have done this."

"The girl needs to know that Liv is her birth mother," Mom said, clenching her jaw. "I'm not going to walk around on eggshells for the next week or more while Liv is getting her act together."

"Liv is my mother?" Miley looked up at Zane, a thousand questions in her beautiful blue eyes.

"Baby," Zane said, picking Miley up, "we need to talk. Everything will be all right."

Alexis ran to her dad and wrapped her arms around his leg, looking at everyone else like they were some kind of foreign monsters.

And Liv didn't blame her.

Zane didn't wait for anyone's permission. He left the main room with Miley in his arms and Alexis clinging to the hem of his shirt. As he walked up the stairs, Miley looked at Liv over her dad's shoulder.

The look tore Liv's heart in two.

Miley clung to Zane's neck, her tears wetting his shoulder. She sobbed as they entered their suite. Alexis had also started to cry, though Zane was certain she didn't really understand what was happening.

"It's okay, sweetheart," Zane said as he rubbed Miley's back. "It's okay, I promise."

He pushed their door closed with his foot and carried Miley to the couch. She didn't loosen her hold, but clung to him tighter as he took a seat.

Alexis crawled up next to him and he put his free arm around his younger daughter. Her eyes were large with tears and worry. She put her thumb in her mouth, and for the first time in a long time, he didn't pull it out.

For several minutes, he just held the girls, allowing them to cry. Miley would have dozens of questions and Zane would answer every single one, to the best of his ability.

Sadness and grief mixed with the surge of anger churning in his gut. Marilyn had no right to tell Miley. She had not only devastated Miley, but she had stolen Liv's opportunity to tell their daughter the truth, in her own way, and in her own time. Zane's heart broke for Miley, but it also broke for Liv. No doubt she was feeling responsible for this debacle and reeling from the way Miley had reacted.

What had Marilyn expected? That Miley would be thrilled to learn the truth, in front of everyone? What had she been thinking? Or *had* she been thinking? As soon as Miley was settled, Zane would have it out with Marilyn once and for all. The woman needed boundaries or a future relationship with her wouldn't be possible.

Finally, Miley's tears began to subside, but she still lay against Zane's chest. It had been a long time since his daughter had sat in his lap.

"What did Grammy mean?" Miley finally whispered.

Zane had wanted Liv to be here for this moment, but he would not make Miley wait.

She deserved to have his complete honesty. "Liv used to be my girlfriend in high school. We loved each other very much and found out we were going to have a baby."

"That was me?" Miley asked.

"That was you." He hugged her close. "But we were very young and scared and didn't know what to do. We never wanted to hurt you, Miley."

"I know, Daddy," she said gently. "What happened?"

His heart squeezed with love for his daughter. "Liv didn't think she could raise a baby."

"Why not?"

"She was young, like I said." How did he tell Miley that Grammy and Grampy had forced Liv to give her away without making them sound like villains? At the moment, he didn't really care if Miley thought poorly of Marilyn, because of the way she had acted, but no matter what, Marilyn would always be Miley's grandmother. At some point, they would have to navigate a tumultuous relationship, and he didn't want to be a stumbling block in his daughter's way.

"Grampy and Grammy thought it would be best for Liv if she gave you to me." Miley didn't need to know about the failed adoption.

That would only hurt her more. "So, I agreed to take you with me. Then, when you were about a year old, I met your mama, Tanya. She loved you so much, Miley. It didn't matter to her that you had a different birth mom. Tanya became your mom in every single way that matters."

More tears filled Miley's eyes and she burrowed her head into Zane's chest.

Alexis looked up at Zane and pulled her thumb out of her mouth long enough to say, "Is Liv my mom?"

"No, baby." Zane kissed the top of her head. "You were born after your mama and I got married."

"Alexis and I have different moms?" Miley's face scrunched up with further heartbreak.

"You have different birth moms." Zane knew it wouldn't be easy to tell Miley the truth. Why had they not been honest with her from the beginning? "But Tanya was your mama, just as much as she was Alexis's. And you both have the same daddy."

"Why didn't Liv want to meet me before?" Miley asked.

"After she gave you to me, we both went on with our lives. She wanted to meet you, but she didn't know where we were living. She has always loved you very much, Miley."

"Why didn't she tell me when we got here?"

"She was waiting until you knew her better. She wanted to tell you today, in private, but Grammy decided to do it without asking permission. I'm very sorry, sweetie. Liv and I wanted you to know, but we didn't want you to find out the way it happened."

Miley was still holding the yellow tutu and she looked down at it now, touching the gold sequins.

Zane held his breath, uncertain of how Miley felt about Liv. No doubt she was confused and hurt, but was she angry? Would she be willing to talk to Liv?

Without warning, Miley threw the tutu across the room. It hit the wall and slid to the ground in a yellow pile of gauzy material.

Miley began to sob again, but this time, she climbed off Zane's lap and ran into her room. She closed the door and locked it.

The clock on the mantel ticked loudly. He didn't allow Miley or Alexis to throw tantrums, but he understood his daughter's need to let out all her pain, so he wouldn't scold her.

A little hand reached up and touched Zane's cheek. Alexis looked up at him, her brown eyes full of understanding beyond her years, and she said, "It will be okay, Daddy." It was what Zane had said to her and Miley a hundred times before.

"It will be," he nodded and pulled her onto his lap for a hug. "Do you know why?"

"Because you love us."

"Exactly."

He sighed, knowing it was time to leave Lakepoint Lodge. They had planned to stay another week and leave the day after New Year's, but he and the girls had overstayed their welcome. He couldn't imagine lingering any longer than necessary after what had just happened. He'd been looking at several different towns in the area and had narrowed down two choices. Both had great school districts and lots of outdoor activities to keep him and the girls busy throughout the year.

But the one that interested him the most was Timber Falls—the very town where Liv had been living for the past decade. He hadn't spoken to her about their future plans, putting it off until they had shared the news with Miley. Would she want him and the girls so close?

Zane wasn't sure if now was the best time to discuss such things with Liv, but if he wanted to leave Lakepoint Lodge, he would need to find a place for him and the girls to go. He couldn't wait much longer.

Chapter Ten

Liv had never been angrier or more upset in her life. Her pulse raced and her body hummed with indignation.

"No one needs to leave," Mom said as Megan and Rachel started to gather the children and take them out of the main room. "We're not done opening gifts."

"I think we need a break right now," Charlie said as he glanced in Liv's direction.

"No." Mom shook her head. "I won't let this ruin my Christmas."

"Ruin *your* Christmas?" Liv could no longer hold in the rage she felt toward her mother. "What about Miley's Christmas or Zane's Christmas? What about Alexis?"

"It's not my fault he wasn't honest with that child from the beginning." Mom stood defiant and Liv knew she would defend her actions and justify her behavior, no matter the cost.

"You had no right," Liv said. "None. Miley is not your daughter. She's mine." The words caught in her throat as emotions rose up to choke her. "And you've hurt her more than anyone ever could."

"No, Olivia." Mom's lips pressed hard and her eyes flashed. "You've hurt her more than anyone ever could."

Pain seared through Liv's chest.

"If anyone is to blame," Mom said, "it's you."

Megan and Rachel rushed the kids out of the room and closed the door behind them.

Charlie, Ben and Dad stayed, but they didn't say a word.

"If you hadn't been so careless, none of this would have happened." Mom sat hard on a rocking chair and crossed her legs and arms. "You were an embarrassment to me. Do you know that? Not only did you ruin your life and Miley's life, you did a fine job trying to ruin my life, as well."

"That's what it's always been about," Liv said. "You didn't force me to give up Miley because it was the best thing for me or her. You thought it would be best for you."

"It was best for all of us."

"Marilyn." There was a warning in Dad's voice. "Enough is enough. You don't mean these things. You're just upset."

"I think she does mean them," Liv said. She turned to her mom. "And they're true. I did a horrible thing eleven years ago, but you did a horrible thing five minutes ago. You were mean-hearted and selfish, and if you can't see that, then I feel sorry for you."

Mom didn't look at Liv but stared out the window. The sun was filling the sky with light and there was a pink tinge on the horizon.

"I had wanted this to work," Liv continued, looking at her dad and brothers and then her mom again. "Even though I don't deserve this, God—and Zane—have given me a second opportunity to do the right thing. I want to be a part of Miley's life, and I wanted to be the one to tell her the truth. You took that right away from me." Her chest was rising and falling on each quick, short breath. "Eleven years ago, I was forced to give up my daughter. Today, I'm going to force you to make a choice. You either love Miley and Alexis like they're your own grandchildren, and treat them with the love and kindness they deserve, or our relationship will come to an end today. I will no longer choose to please you over doing what is best for my daughter."

A hush fell over the family as Mom's mouth slipped open and she turned to look at Liv.

"You should think very carefully before you speak, Marilyn," Dad said. "Because I've already made my decision. Miley is our granddaughter and I will love her until the day I die."

Mom looked sharply at Dad and then her gaze traveled over to Ben and Charlie. They were both staring at her with hard, steady gazes. Liv knew that she had her brothers' and father's support, but she wasn't so sure of her Mom. Marilyn Butler had been a force to reckon with since Liv was a child. There had been good times—and many wonderful memories—but whenever her mother didn't get her way, she retaliated. Liv had watched her lose several friends over the years because of her stubbornness and her inability to apologize or admit she was wrong.

Would she make the same mistake now? Or would she take this seriously and realize what was at stake?

No one spoke, and Liv's breathing began to normalize again. The next few moments would have lasting consequences on their family for years to come.

"I'm sorry, Olivia," Mom said quietly. She uncrossed her arms and legs and stood. "I shouldn't have done what I did. Both you and Miley deserve better."

Liv stared at her mom, speechless. She could count the times on her right hand that her mom had apologized for her behavior.

"I was upset, like your dad said, and I tend to say things I regret when I'm mad." She walked across the room and came to stand before Liv. "Your dad and I thought we were doing the best thing for you eleven years ago, but I'm starting to realize that we could have been wrong. I had no idea how much you were hurting all these years. And the last thing I want is to lose you, like you lost Miley."

Tears stung Liv's eyes, and she had to blink several times to stop them from falling down her cheeks. For years, she had avoided her mother. She hadn't ever thought that standing up to her would actually work.

"Will you forgive me?" Mom asked.

For the first time in a long time, a surge of affection filled Liv's heart for her mother. Liv had given up on her long ago, but today was proof that no one was beyond redemption.

"Of course I forgive you, Mom." She hugged her mother and realized it had been a long time since they'd been this close. "But I can't let you hurt Miley again. I need to trust that you will let Zane and I make the best choices for her, or we won't be able to spend time with you."

Her mom hugged her tighter. "You're right. Of course you're right." She pulled back and looked into Liv's eyes. "I promise I won't overstep my boundaries again."

Liv wanted to believe her mother, but a lot of past hurt would take a long time to heal. Her mother would have to prove she was worthy of Liv's trust again.

"I hope so."

Dad joined them and put his arm around Liv. "I will see that she keeps her promise, because I'm not ready to say goodbye to you, Miley or Alexis anytime soon."

"Liv, maybe you should go up and talk to Zane and Miley," Charlie suggested.

"I don't know if I'll be welcome up there." It still hurt that Liv hadn't been the one to tell Miley. She'd been thinking about it for the past few days and had already decided how she would do it. Now it was all ruined. Even though her mom apologized, she was still angry and frustrated at how it had all come about.

"You need to at least try," Dad said.

He was right. Liv didn't want her and Miley to have a relationship like her and her mother. Communication was so important, and it would need to start now. Even if it would be hard.

Her legs were shaky as she walked up the staircase. She held on to the handrail for support and stopped just outside Zane's door.

What was she going to say? How would she face Miley?

She knocked on the door and noticed her hand shaking just as much as her legs.

A few seconds later, Zane opened the door, but he didn't move aside to welcome her in.

It didn't take long for Liv to see past him and notice that Miley was not in the living space, and the tutu was lying in a heap against the wall. Alexis was sitting on the couch, her large brown eyes wary at Liv's arrival, as she sucked her thumb.

"I'm so sorry, Zane." Liv finally met his gaze. Her voice was wobbly with emotion. "I don't even know where to begin—"

"It wasn't your fault." His voice was hard and stiff and even though he told her it wasn't her fault, it felt like it was.

"I feel awful." She pressed her lips together to stop them from trembling. "How is she?"

"She's hurt and confused." His face softened with sadness. "And she's angry."

Liv closed her eyes briefly. Of course she was angry.

"I think it's time I get packed up and leave," Zane said.

"Leave?" Liv's heart dropped. She wasn't ready to say goodbye to them. "But it's Christmas. You shouldn't have to go anywhere on Christmas."

"I don't think I can stay here after what happened."

"Where will you go?"

"Probably to a hotel for a few nights until I can find a place to rent. It's not easy around the holidays." He looked like he was going to say something more, but he closed his mouth.

"I don't want you to go."

"Your mom did the unthinkable, Liv. I can't stay here if she's going to blatantly hurt my children."

"Of course you can't." Liv wanted to tell Zane her mom had apologized, but she knew it would need to come from her mom if it was going to make a difference to Zane. "I completely understand."

They stood there for a moment, neither one speaking, and then Zane said, "I should probably start packing."

Liv didn't know what to say. She wanted to beg him not to go, but the truth was, she didn't feel like staying, either. Especially if Zane and the girls left.

"I'll bring something for you and the girls to eat." She paused and her heart beat faster. "Do you think Miley would be willing to talk to me before you leave?"

Zane looked toward the closed bedroom door and shrugged. "I couldn't really say."

"Okay." Liv nodded. "I'll let her take as long as she needs, but can you please tell her that when she's ready, I'd like to talk to her?"

"Of course I can."

Liv left their room and started toward the stairs again, knowing that Zane would be gone if her mother didn't apologize.

But would an apology be enough to fix the trouble her mother had created?

An hour later, Alexis was asleep on the couch and Miley still hadn't come out of her room. Zane stood near the window in his bedroom and looked out at the frozen lake. He'd only arrived at Lakepoint Lodge with the girls five days ago, yet it felt like a lifetime. It seemed unreal that it had been less than a week since they'd been in Europe. Where might they be in a week from now?

The suitcase was open on his bed, but he hadn't packed much. He had every intention of leaving, but he didn't want to rush Miley out the door before she was ready to face everyone again. It wouldn't be right to slip out the back door without saying goodbye, even if that's exactly what he wanted to do.

He had looked online to see if there was a hotel available close by, but he hadn't made any reservations. Most things were booked up for the holidays, and the closest one with availability was an hour's drive away.

A knock sounded on the door in the living space. Liv had already brought up a tray of food, but she hadn't stayed long, since Miley was still in her room and Alexis had been sleepy. He had noticed the tears staining her face and had suspected she needed a little bit of time to herself.

Had she come back to talk?

Zane's heart beat a little faster as he left his room and went to the door. When he pulled it open, he was surprised to see Marilyn standing in the hallway.

A rush of anger pulsed through Zane's veins. What did she want? To cause more pain and heartache, to force them to leave before they were ready?

He gripped the doorknob and braced his feet, ready for an attack.

Marilyn stood alone, with her hands clasped together. She glanced around Zane and then said, quietly, "Is this a good time to talk?"

Was there ever a good time to talk with Marilyn? He didn't respond but kept staring at her, afraid that if he opened his mouth to speak, he'd say something he would regret.

"I'd like to talk to you, if I could." She took a step back into the hallway. "In private."

At least she had the decency to suggest a bit of privacy. Why hadn't she been concerned about what the girls might hear before?

Zane left the suite and closed the door behind him. He remembered, in vivid clarity, stepping into the hall with Liv five days ago, having one of the hardest conversations of his life. He had known dealing with her family would be difficult, but he hadn't imagined how tough it would be or how much it would upset Miley.

Marilyn swallowed as she twisted her hands together. "I've come to apologize, Zane. What I did was inexcusable and selfish. I thought that by breaking the ice and telling Miley the truth it would force Liv to deal with reality, but I now realize I was wrong. I should have let you and Liv do what you felt best, but I thought you were taking too long and I didn't think it was fair to Miley." She was rambling and it was clear she was uncomfortable, but Zane didn't make a move to ease her discomfort. "I guess what I'm saying is that I'm sorry. I was wrong and it takes a lot for me to admit that."

An awkward silence filled the hall as Zane contemplated what she had said. He remembered talking with Liv about Tanya and how thankful he was that she had offered Tanya grace. Wasn't Zane obligated to offer the same grace and forgiveness to Marilyn? Even if it was hard, and even if it didn't make all their troubles go away?

"Will you accept my apology, Zane?" Marilyn asked. "I know it won't fix things, but I've apologized to Liv and I've promised her I won't overstep my boundaries again."

"You've already talked to Liv?"

She nodded, her face lined with regret. "I've also apologized to the rest of the family. I plan to do everything I can to make this right."

"I don't know if you can make this right, Marilyn." Zane's voice was thick with emotions he was still trying to contain. "You've hurt Miley deeply. This isn't something that can be easily fixed."

"I understand that now." She let out a weary sigh. "I know there are a lot of wounds that will take time to heal, but I want to do my part to see that our family is healthy and whole once again." She worked her mouth back and forth for a moment, and Zane wondered if she was going to cry. He couldn't handle more tears today. "I have finally realized that what I did to Liv eleven years ago wasn't the best choice we could have made. At the time, I was embarrassed and angry. I wasn't thinking correctly. I was only thinking about her future—or, at least, the one I had imagined—and a teen pregnancy was not how I envisioned that future starting. I wanted to make the problem go away—and I thought I had—but now I see it only made things worse."

Zane put himself in Marilyn's shoes and thought about Miley and Alexis. He would like to think he would help his daughters navigate hard times better than Marilyn had, but he was smart enough to know he would also be very disappointed and upset if one of his girls came to him at the age of seventeen, expecting a child. He wasn't perfect. Hadn't he messed up with Tanya when she had come to him, upset and wanting to leave Rome? If he didn't handle this situation with Marilyn better, would he one day regret not accepting her apology? This was about more than him. He had Miley, Alexis and Liv to think about, too. If he couldn't get past this trouble, how could they move forward?

"What do you think?" Marilyn asked, her eyebrows raised in cautious hope. "I know I don't deserve it, but I'd like your forgiveness and the chance to start over."

Taking a deep breath, Zane nodded. "Of course I forgive you. But I need you to know that I cannot—and will not—let you hurt Miley again. If I perceive any hostility or harm coming her way, you won't see her again. I hate to be so hard, but she is my number-one priority."

"Of course." Marilyn nodded. "I understand completely."

He adjusted his stance and said, "I also need to ask you to accept *my* apology."

"Your apology?"

"I don't think I've ever said how sorry I am for what all of you went through. I am just as much to blame as anyone."

Marilyn shook her head. "It's behind us now. We can't change the past, but we can move forward and change the future."

Zane nodded. She was right.

"Liv said you are planning to leave." She

frowned, clearly sad at the idea. "I hope you'll consider staying for the rest of the week. We have some fun things planned and I know everyone—including me—would be sad to see you leave."

"I don't know if it's a good idea, given the circumstances."

"Oh, please think about it. I'm going to make a huge Christmas meal and we want you to stay and enjoy it with us. The kids have loved getting to know Miley and Alexis, and I know how much it would mean to Liv if you stayed."

Zane shook his head. "It will all depend on Miley. I won't make her stay if she doesn't want to."

Disappointment tilted Marilyn's eyebrows, but she nodded. "I understand."

"When she's ready, I'll talk to her again and see what she wants to do. I'll let you know as soon as I'm able."

"Okay." Marilyn continued to nod. "Just know that you're welcome to stay."

"I appreciate that."

Marilyn turned and walked to the staircase.

Zane reentered his suite and went to Miley's bedroom door. He stood for a moment, offering up a silent prayer for his daughter and for himself. He needed the right words to speak to her heart, because he knew that whatever he said would go a long way in determining how she processed her new reality. The last thing he wanted was to cause her more pain and confusion. He wouldn't pressure her to stay, but he wouldn't encourage her to leave, either. No matter what, he wanted to listen to her needs and guide her on her path to understanding.

He hesitated for another moment and then knocked lightly. "Miley?" he called. "May I come in?"

She didn't respond, so he knocked again.

"Miley? It's Daddy. I'd like to come in and talk to you."

A movement in the room told him Miley was awake and a second later, the door opened.

Her face was swollen and her eyes were red, but at least she had let him in. If that was all she would allow right now, it would have to be enough.

Chapter Eleven

"Hi, Daddy."

"Hey, baby."

Miley reached for him and he picked her up. At the age of eleven, she hadn't been held like this in years, but she was light and if she needed to be held, he would hold her.

He walked over to a chair near the window and sat down.

Sunshine lit up the whole room. Outside the window, the day looked crisp and inviting, with a bright blue sky and no clouds in sight.

Zane held Miley, not wanting to rush her. He remembered the hours and hours they had sat in this very same position, after Tanya had died, when both of them had been crying and asking questions that didn't have answers.

But this time was so much different than

the last. When Tanya had died, it had been an accident, and there had been no one to blame. This time, the blame was on Zane's shoulders for choosing not to tell Miley the truth from the very beginning. And Marilyn's shoulders for sharing it in such a traumatic way. Miley's tears tore at Zane's heart, because he knew he could have done something to change this outcome if he'd only been smarter and wiser in the past.

"Why didn't you tell me before?" she finally asked, looking up at him. Her eyes looked bluer than ever.

It was a simple question and he wished he had a simple answer.

"You were a year old when I met Tanya," he finally said. "You two loved each other immediately. So much so I used to be afraid that Tanya liked you more than me."

A small smile tilted up Miley's lips—the first hint of restoration.

"You were inseparable from day one, and when Tanya and I got engaged and she knew she was going to be your mommy, she asked if you could call her mom. You were only eighteen months old, so I didn't see any harm in it. It actually made a lot of sense. By the time we got married, you were five, and you were her daughter in every single way possible. As you grew, we never found a good time to tell you the truth. And then when she died, I didn't want to add more pain to your grief."

"Did you bring me here to meet Liv?"

"No." Zane shook his head and repositioned Miley so he could see her face better. "God brought us here—I'm certain of it. I didn't know Liv was going to be here, and she didn't know I was coming."

"Didn't you want me to meet her?"

Zane shrugged. "I don't know, really. The last thing I wanted was for you to get hurt. I didn't seek out Liv, because I didn't know if she wanted to meet you, but I quickly realized she did." He wanted to help Liv and Miley as much as possible, so he said, "Liv has been very sad since the day she gave you to me. It was the hardest thing she's ever done, Miley. She didn't give you to me because she wanted to. She gave you to me because she thought it would be the best thing for you. I told you she was very young. But now she's grown up, and she wants you to be a part of her life, if you want it, too."

Miley picked at a loose thread on Zane's sweater and stared at it for a moment.

"She came up here earlier," he continued. "But I told her we need to give you some time to process everything you've learned before she talks to you."

"What does she want to say?"

"I don't know." He touched her cheek. "What I *do* know is that she loves you with all her heart, and she will wait as long as it takes for you to be ready."

Miley glanced outside the window and then looked back at Zane. "We didn't finish opening up our presents."

He smiled, loving her childish resiliency. It was just like her to be concerned about gifts at a time like now. "I wasn't sure if you wanted to stay and keep celebrating Christmas. There is a hotel we can go to if you'd like to leave."

She took a deep breath and shook her head. "I don't want to go. I like Kendra and the other kids."

"They're your cousins, you know."

Her eyes opened wide and she smiled. "Kendra's my cousin?"

"Yes." He laughed. "And so are Leah, Jackson, Nicole and Anders. Megan and Rachel are also your aunts."

Miley's smile faded. "Then that means Grammy is—"

"Your grandmother." He took one of her hands in his. It was so small and delicate. At some point, she had painted her nails red with one of the cousins. "Grammy came up here just a little while ago to tell me—and you—that she's very sorry for what she did. She admits she was wrong and wants us to know she will do a better job. And we're welcome to stay for the rest of the week, if we'd like."

There was a quiet pause as Miley played with Zane's hand. "I like Grampy," she said.

"And Grampy likes you. They all love you, Miley. You and Alexis."

"But Kendra isn't Alexis's cousin?" she asked.

"No—not really—but they will all treat her as a cousin."

Again, there was silence as Miley worked through all the things Zane had told her.

"I won't make you stay," he said, "but, if you'd like, we don't need to leave. We can keep celebrating Christmas here. It's up to you."

"Okay." Miley nodded. "I think I'd like to stay."

"Are you sure?"

"Yes."

"Are you ready to go back downstairs and see everyone?"

"Mmm." She pressed her mouth together as she thought. "Everyone but Grammy."

"I don't think we can avoid her. If we stay, we'll have to see everyone, but she will be a lot nicer from now on." He would make sure of it.

Miley sighed. "All right."

Zane hugged his daughter close. "I'm so proud of you, Miley. We can't always control what happens to us, but we can control how we respond to each situation. You've gone through a lot of heartache, but you still keep a smile on your face and you offer forgiveness so easily. That's an amazing gift. One I pray you will continue to use throughout the rest of your life."

Her big blue eyes searched his face when she pulled back, and she offered him one of her sweetest smiles.

They had overcome a lot of hurdles in a short time, but one of the biggest was yet to come.

"Before we rejoin everyone, I think you and Liv should see each other. Are you ready to talk to her?"

Miley bit the inside of her mouth in a familiar sign of nerves. "Will you come with me?"

"Of course I will, if that's what you want. I will never leave you alone to deal with these big issues, unless you want to be alone."

"Thank you, Daddy."

"Are you ready now?"

"I think so."

Alexis was still asleep in the other room, which would give them the best opportunity to meet with Liv alone. Yet, he didn't want to leave Alexis, in case she woke up while they were gone and got scared. She'd already suffered enough trauma today.

"How about I call Liv and ask her to come to our room?"

Miley nodded and then climbed off Zane's lap. They walked into the living space, and while Zane retrieved his phone, Miley went to the tutu lying on the ground.

Ever so gently, she picked it up and held it in her arms.

It was hard to read her thoughts as she studied the garment, but Zane was sure of one thing about this strong and beautiful daughter of his: she wouldn't toss it away a second time.

There was a heaviness unlike anything Liv had ever felt weighing upon her heart. It was so strong it felt like a physical force, pressing the breath out of her lungs. She'd experienced something like it once before, when she'd walked away from Miley in the hospital, but this time it was different.

Miley knew Liv was her birth mother and the stakes were higher. Would Miley reject her? Would she hate her? Worse, would *Miley* feel rejected by Liv? Eleven years ago, the baby she had given up didn't have a name or a personality. At the time, Liv could only imagine what her daughter would grow up to look like and what she would enjoy. There had been a lot of questions, but, for the most part, every time she had thought about her daughter, there had been a void in her mind.

But not anymore. Miley had filled all the voided places, answered almost all the questions and surprised Liv with the intensity of the love she felt for her daughter. No longer was Miley an unknown entity. The threat of losing her was far worse than the threat of never knowing her.

A quick glance at the clock next to the bed told Liv it was late morning. Zane was probably packing his suitcases, preparing to leave at any moment.

Liv was doing the same. Though she had accepted her mother's apology, she wasn't prepared to stay at the resort when Zane left. She would head back to Timber Falls and bury herself in her work. She'd done it before and she could do it again. Work was the only thing she could depend on. It was there, waiting for her like an old companion. Though it left a lot to be desired, at least it was steady and controllable.

Her cell phone started to vibrate on the nightstand. Liv didn't feel like speaking to anyone, so she went to turn it off and saw Zane's name on the screen.

Her hands began to shake all over again, and her stomach did a little flip. Was he calling to tell her he was leaving? She had spoken to her mother and asked her to apologize to Zane, but Liv hadn't waited around to see if she would. She needed to be alone, so she had come to her room to pack.

Even if Mom had apologized, would Zane be willing to stay?

Liv was almost certain he wouldn't.

"Hello," she said into the phone.

"Hey, Liv." Zane's voice was so calm and steady, like a gentle balm to her weary soul. She would miss him—more now than ever—when they were forced to return to their daily lives.

How would she be patient between visits with him and the girls? That is if he was still willing to let her visit them.

"Are you busy?" he asked.

"I'm just packing my bags."

There was a pause. "Are you leaving?"

"I think it's the best thing to do." She walked to the window in her bedroom and looked out at the frozen lake. Ice houses dotted the snow-covered surface, and there were a few trucks parked next to them.

Again, he paused. "I've spoken to Miley and I think she's ready to talk to you."

A rush of nervous energy surged through Liv and she felt like she might be sick. This was the moment she'd been waiting for. She would finally face her daughter, with Miley knowing the truth. It was both frightening and liberating at the same time.

"Would you like to talk to her?" he asked.

"Yes," she said quickly.

"Can you come to our room? Alexis is still asleep, and I don't want to leave her here alone."

"Of course I can come. I'll be there in a couple seconds."

"You're okay if I'm here while you talk?"

She hadn't contemplated having him there, but it only made sense. Ever since he'd shown up in her life again, she had felt like they were a team. She didn't need to face this challenge on her own, and the reality of it almost made her cry. It had been a long time since she'd felt so connected to another person. "Yes. I would appreciate you being there."

Suddenly, she was nervous about her appearance—more so than if she was going on a blind date or being interviewed on national television. After she hung up the phone, she looked in the mirror and saw that her eyes were red from crying and there were worry lines creasing her mouth. After removing the messy bun she'd haphazardly thrown in while she was packing, she shook out her blond hair and ran her hands through it a few times. She didn't want to take time to change, but she was wearing yoga pants and a baggy sweatshirt—not exactly the clothes she'd imagined herself wearing while talking to her daughter for the first time—at least, for the first time her daughter really knew who she was.

But none of that mattered. Would Miley even care what she was wearing? And she was wasting precious time. For all she knew, Zane and the girls were already dressed in their coats and hats, waiting to leave.

With that alarming thought, Liv left her suite and walked the short distance to Zane's. She took a deep breath, praying for wisdom and peace, and then knocked on the door.

Zane opened it a moment later, wearing his black-rimmed glasses, his chin still covered in a shadow of a beard. He wasn't wearing his outdoor clothes and there were no suitcases waiting by the door.

Liv breathed a sigh of relief. At least, for now, she had more time with him and the girls.

His very presence eased Liv's nerves, but only a little. Though he offered her a gentle smile, there was concern and tension around his eyes. "Thanks for coming," he said.

"Are you sure she's ready to talk to me?"

"I think so." He nodded toward Alexis, snuggled up on the couch. "I thought we could talk in Miley's room, so Alexis can keep sleeping. Miley's waiting for us."

Liv nodded, her entire body trembling with the knowledge that she was about to face their daughter.

Zane closed the suite door and then he put his hand on Liv's arm. "You don't need to be afraid."

"Is it that obvious?"

"Your face is white and you're trembling all over. You also look like you're about to be sick." He gently cupped Liv's elbow and turned her to face him. "The most important thing Miley needs to know is that you love her, Liv. The rest will fall into place."

"I wish it was that simple."

"It really is." His other hand went over her other elbow and he smiled at her. "Just take a couple deep breaths." He took one with her. "I'll be there with you the whole time, and I can promise you Miley will offer you more grace and forgiveness than you're prepared to offer yourself."

"Thank you," she said.

"You should also know that I didn't tell her that we had planned to give her up for adoption. I didn't think it necessary to add that to her heartache right now." He ran his hands up and down the backs of her arms, an encouraging smile on his face.

She nodded, thankful she knew that bit of information.

"Ready?" he asked.

She took a deep breath and followed him to Miley's door. He knocked and then opened it so Liv could walk inside.

Miley was sitting on the end of her bed, the yellow tutu in her lap. Her tears were dried, but her face was still a little red and puffy from crying.

When she looked up at Liv, her emotions were hard to read, but she did not look angry or hurt. Instead, she looked curious.

Zane gently closed the door behind him and then pulled a chair away from the desk for Liv to sit on. He grabbed a second chair from another corner of the room, and the three of them sat in a sort of circle.

Liv was thankful for the chair, since she didn't think her wobbly legs would hold her up for much longer.

The three of them sat for a few moments in silence, and Liv was uncertain where to begin. She'd imagined this moment for years, yet she couldn't think of a single thing to say.

"Daddy told me," Miley said to Liv, breaking the silence.

It was all she needed to say. "I'm so very sorry, Miley." Tears threatened to fall, but Liv forced them back. If she started now, she'd never stop, and this conversation was too important to mess up. "I'm sorry for what happened today, but I'm even more sorry for not being there for you these past eleven years."

"Daddy told me you were young and afraid when you had me." Miley watched Liv openly, as if waiting for Liv to confirm or deny what Zane had told her.

"He's right." She let out a breath—one she felt like she'd been holding for eleven years. She wanted to tell her daughter everything—from the moment she'd delivered her until the moment she'd met her in the parking lot—yet, it would be impossible to sum it all up in one simple conversation. Instead, she told her the most important parts. "The saddest day of my life was the day I handed you over to the nurse and knew that I would never get to see you again." She forced the tears back one more time. "I didn't think God would allow me to meet you and get to know you, but He did, and it's the greatest gift I've ever received. I never wanted to hurt you."

"I know." She didn't move as she sat on the bed, but her little hand absently played with the sequins on the tutu. "Daddy told me you thought you were doing the best thing for me."

She was giving Liv so much mercy, and Liv was certain she didn't deserve it. She had thought talking to Miley would be hard, yet, Miley was easing the way, and she loved her all the more for it.

"When I met you, just last week," Liv continued, "and I saw what a good job your daddy had done raising you, I knew I had nothing to worry about." She met Zane's gaze and saw so much tenderness there she had to look away. "I would have given anything to be with you and watch you grow up, but knowing that your daddy and your mama loved you so well makes my heart very glad."

"Did you love my daddy when you had

me?" Her question was so unexpected, and so innocent, Liv was taken aback for a second. But she knew the answer and would give it to Miley freely.

"I did love your daddy. Very much." She couldn't look at Zane, afraid she'd give too much away. Her love for him had not ended the day they had parted ways. It hadn't been her choice to call it off.

Miley nodded and smiled. "He loved you, too. I know it."

Liv finally glanced at Zane. He took his gaze off Miley and looked at Liv. There were so many emotions flooding her senses she was afraid to even contemplate what he might be thinking.

"The most important thing for you to know," Liv continued, looking back at Miley, "is that both of us loved you then and we love you now. If you have any questions, you can always ask me or your daddy. I won't ever keep anything from you again. I promise."

"Will I see you when we leave here?" Miley asked.

"If you'd like to see me."

"Every day?"

Liv looked at Zane again, questions in her eyes. Would it be possible? "That all depends on where you live," she finally said to Miley.

"I would love to see you every day, but if we live too far apart, then I will come to you whenever I get the chance. But I'll be there for you, no matter what happens."

Just the thought of being involved in Miley's life made Liv's chest fill to capacity with love and joy. She didn't deserve to be a part of her daughter's life, but by some beautiful blessing from God, she would have the opportunity.

"Does this sound okay to you?" Zane asked Miley.

Miley finally offered Liv the first smile since she had entered her room. She nodded. "Yes."

Liv couldn't hide her smile, which was just as wide as her daughter's.

"Can we go and open the rest of our presents now?" Miley asked Zane.

"If that's what you'd like to do."

"Yes, please." She bounded off her bed and started for the door, but then she came back and picked up the tutu. "Can I wear this?" she asked Liv.

"It's yours," Liv said. "You may do whatever you'd like with it, sweetheart."

"Okay." Miley smiled again and then left the room.

Liv stayed in her chair, too overcome to get to her feet.

Zane reached over and took one of her hands into his. It was gentle and sweet and caused her to look up at him. "It's just the beginning," he said. "The first conversation of many that will span the rest of your life. We still have a long road ahead of us." He smiled, his gaze both teasing and serious at the same time. "Braces, driver's tests, boyfriends, math homework. But if you'd like to be a part of it all, I'd like to find a way to make it work."

Her pulse skipped a beat, but she managed to nod.

He let go of her hand and leaned back in his chair. "I found a house to rent in Timber Falls, but I don't want to—"

"Timber Falls?" Her voice caught as she stared at him. "You'd move to Timber Falls for me?"

"For you and Miley." He studied her. "I can live pretty much wherever I want, but it doesn't make any sense to put distance between you and Miley. She'll have school programs and parent/teacher conferences and so many other things. I don't want you to have to miss a single thing."

Her heart expanded so much her chest felt tight with love and appreciation for Zane Harris. "Zane, there's no way I could possibly repay you for your thoughtfulness. I don't deserve it."

"She's your daughter, Liv. And you've missed far too much already. It's the least I can do."

"No." She shook her head. "It's more than I could ever hope for or imagine."

"Are you prepared to tell your friends and neighbors about her?"

"I can't think of anything I want more." She paused. "Except one thing."

"What's that?" He leaned forward.

"Could I go to Alexis's school programs, too?"

Zane's grin was bigger than she'd ever seen and he laughed. "I'd love that."

So would Liv.

Chapter Twelve

The noise in the resort's dining room was louder and more rambunctious than ever before. Zane sat at the adult table, the Christmas meal spread out before him, and watched Miley interact with her cousins at the children's table. She was laughing and joking with them in a way she hadn't before. He had watched her link arms with Kendra and put their heads together on more than one occasion to whisper.

It felt good to see her bonding with her cousins. She had a few older ones on his side of the family that they didn't see often, and Tanya's only sister didn't have children. This gift was yet one more Zane would add to the list of things to be grateful for.

He caught Liv's eyes and offered her a smile. She was sitting across from him, like usual, but this time, there were no more secrets between them and Miley. It was refreshing to have it all out in the open—even if it hadn't been easy, and there were still a lot of unanswered questions regarding the future.

The most pressing was how they would share time with Miley. Would they have a formal agreement, or would it come about naturally? How much did Liv want to see Zane while she spent time with Miley and Alexis, since he already knew she wanted to be involved in Alexis's life as much as Miley's?

"We have one more Christmas surprise," Marilyn said to the room as she stood from her spot at the end of the table.

Zane glanced at Liv with apprehension. Her mother had already given away one too many surprises today, and the adults were still reeling from the awkwardness. It was receding, little by little, but it was still there in the stilted conversation and sideways glances. Everyone was doing their best to ease the tension, but it would probably take the rest of the week to settle back into a bit of normalcy.

"Another present?" Jackson asked.

"Sort of." Marilyn wiggled her eyebrows in anticipation. "But I won't tell you what it is until we've cleaned up the dining room and everyone has their winter clothes on."

The kids chattered as they cleared their plates off the table and brought them into the kitchen.

"Let's start washing the dishes for Grammy," Miley said to Kendra.

"Okay."

"Wow," Megan said to Zane as she started to stack the adult plates. "I'm impressed."

"Don't let her fool you," Zane responded. "She's only doing it so they can get to their surprise faster."

The meal had been amazing. Roasted turkey, cranberry sauce, mashed potatoes, stuffing and the best apple pie he'd ever eaten. His stomach was full and he was tired. A mixture of the heavy food, the early wake time and the stress of the day had caught up to him. It was already dark outside, though it was only six-thirty. He could have easily found a couch to take a nap.

"Don't forget," Marilyn said as she came up behind Zane and put her hand on his shoulder to reach for a serving dish on the table. "You'll need to wear your warmest outdoor clothes."

What could they be doing outside in the dark?

The whole family worked to get the kitchen and dining room clean. With everyone pitching in, it was done in record time and they were all dressed and standing outside the lodge thirty minutes later.

"Just in time," Marilyn said, her voice at an excited pitch. "Do you hear that?"

Everyone was standing on the deck, chatting, but they quieted down to listen.

"I don't hear anything," Jackson said with a frown. He was only five—Alexis's age—and was a firecracker. Zane had loved getting to know each of the kids, but Jackson's antics were by far his favorite. Rachel and Charlie had shared several stories about the little guy, and Zane had laughed and groaned through each one. By the sounds of it, Jackson kept his parents busy.

"Listen harder," Marilyn instructed the children.

Silence filled the air as everyone strained to hear what she heard.

And then, Zane did hear something. It was the sound of bells, coming from the road.

"I hear jingle bells!" Jackson cried out.

Within moments, a horse-drawn wagon appeared on the road and entered the parking lot. Lanterns hung from both sides of the wagon, casting soft light across the white snow.

"Who wants to go on a wagon ride tonight?" Marilyn asked the children.

"Me, me!" they shouted in unison.

The horses were magnificent. Identical in color and shape, with bells hanging from their harnesses. The driver was an older gentleman wearing a matching plaid coat and hat. He had a thick mustache and held a smoking pipe in hand. "Evening," he called out to them as he pulled his horses to a stop and secured the wagon brake.

Marilyn and Bob went up to speak to the driver while Zane stayed on the deck, next to Liv, watching as the children greeted the horses and clambered onto the back of the wagon.

"This is pretty amazing," he said to Liv. "I'm happy we decided to stay."

"I agree. It would have been sad to miss out on a horse-drawn wagon ride."

"That's not what I'm talking about." He looked down at her, his chest filling with dozens of emotions and feelings—and all of them good. "I'm talking about all of it. The meal, watching Miley with her cousins—and with you."

Her eyes were so beautiful as she met his gaze.

"I love that we don't have the secret hanging over our heads anymore," he continued.

"It makes me feel free in a way I haven't felt in a long time."

"Me, too."

"Daddy!" Miley called out to Zane from the back of the wagon. "Come on. You and Liv will miss the ride."

On instinct, Zane almost reached out to take Liv's hand, but he caught himself at the last moment. Instead, they walked side by side down the steps and reached the wagon together.

Everyone was already on board, and with thirteen people already seated, most of the hay bales were spoken for.

Liv climbed up first and then Zane followed.

"I saved you two a spot right here, by me," Miley said to her parents. She wore a silly smile on her face as she pointed to the spot that was really meant for one person. "You can share."

"It doesn't look big enough for the both of us," Zane said to his daughter. "I'll take the spot up near the front."

"No." Miley shook her head and then nudged one of her cousins to move. "You go up front, Anders," she said to the little boy. "I want my dad and Liv to sit here."

"Say please," Zane said to Miley.

"Please, Anders."

"Come on, buddy," Megan said as she lifted her son off the bale of hay. "You can sit by me and Dad."

Anders didn't protest, so Miley pointed at the two places on either side of her. "One spot for Daddy and one spot for Liv."

Zane glanced at Liv, and though it was dark, he could see how pleased she was with Miley's exuberance to be near her.

Liv sat first, but then Miley jumped up and said, "Daddy, you sit next to Liv."

"You need to make up your mind, Miley," Zane said to his daughter. "The driver wants to get going."

"You should sit next to Liv." She pointed to the spot. Zane took a seat next to her, with Miley on the other side.

As the wagon started to move, Liv pressed into Zane's side, and he didn't mind in the least. He loved feeling her close beside him, smelling the scent of her shampoo, hearing her soft breath as she inhaled the cold air, watching it billow out in a foggy cloud from her mouth.

Miley glanced up at him, a secretive smile on her lips, and he wondered what she was thinking. Was she still hopeful that Zane and Liv would get together? Ever since her cousins had arrived, she hadn't spent much time playing matchmaker. Now that she knew the truth, was it on her mind again?

His heart beat faster at the thought. He hadn't entertained a romantic relationship with Liv because things had been too complicated, but what about now? Other than Miley knowing the truth about Liv, nothing else had changed. He was still a single dad, needing to focus on raising his daughters and getting them settled into a new town and school. Was there room in his life for a girlfriend or wife? More important, was there room for Liv?

The driver brought them onto the road, which was unpopulated and dark on this Christmas evening. Snow-laden branches hung low to the ground, while the stars sparkled above. The air was crisp and fresh. Megan began to sing "O Holy Night," and her clear voice was melodic and soft above the sound of the jingling bells. Soon, the others joined in, and they offered up a beautiful chorus.

Liv was still pressed close to Zane's side, and he had the strongest urge to put his arm around her but refrained. She had given him no sign that she would welcome or encourage his attention. He knew she appreciated him, and maybe even liked him, but he had no idea whether or not she still harbored stronger feelings for him.

And as the horses led them through the silent woods, while the Butler family sang Christmas carols, Zane finally admitted the truth: he longed for Liv to return the feelings he could no longer deny.

The week progressed faster than Liv wanted, but she tried to savor each moment. They roasted marshmallows around a campfire, went ice fishing on the lake, sledded down the big hill and ate the most delicious food Liv had enjoyed since living at home. In the mornings, she and Zane either snowshoed, went cross-country skiing or ran together on the plowed county road. Her mom went out of her way to make the holiday special and memorable, and for that, Liv was thankful. She was good to her word and made Miley and Alexis feel not only welcomed, but an important part of their family.

It was already New Year's Eve. But more important, it was the day of the big hockey game. Ben and Charlie were the team captains and they had recruited everyone, except Mom, to play. She said she would watch from the sidelines and cheer on both teams. Even Jackson and Anders would play, though

Megan and Rachel made the men promise to go easy on them. It would have to be a family friendly game, and since all the children except Miley and Alexis had experience playing hockey, they had agreed.

The sky was cloudy and the forecast called for several inches of snow that evening and into the next day. Everyone was planning on leaving the day after New Year's, since it was a Sunday, so they only had two more days to enjoy each other's company. Mom and Dad would stay at the resort, since it was their full-time residence now, Ben and Charlie would take their families home to Marshall, and Zane would be moving his girls into a rental home just a few blocks away from Liv's house in Timber Falls. Though she was sad to see the holidays end, she was excited about returning home to her new normal. Whatever that might be.

"Ready for some hockey?" Dad asked the two teams as they assembled on the ice. They were fairly even, with roughly the same number of adults and children on each team. Some of the kids had brought their full gear, which they had shared with Miley and Alexis, but the adults opted to not wear any pads or helmets, since there would be little to no contact.

Liv and Zane were on opposite teams and

she met his gaze across the expanse of frozen water. He smiled at her and her heart did a little somersault. All throughout the week, they had spent time together, sharing in the newfound joy of Miley's knowledge. It had bonded them in a way that nothing else could. But more than that, there was a new awareness that she had discovered. With the secret no longer hovering over their heads, they had relaxed with one another, bantering and flirting like they used to do.

And she liked it—a lot.

Yet, she knew she couldn't let it go any further than flirting. She wasn't good at relationships. That broken piece of her heart didn't allow her to have any success with boyfriends. Things always became too complicated, and none were as complicated as her relationship with Zane. How could she possibly start something with him, when things were already difficult? It was better to keep him at a distance and maintain a friendship, rather than allow him to get close and deal with her broken heart.

The game started and Liv soon realized she wasn't as adept at hockey as she was in high school. Her brothers were still a force to be reckoned with and they were good—really good. And so were the kids. All of Ben's and

Charlie's kids had been in hockey since they could walk. Even Jackson and Anders were already playing on the Mini-Mite teams.

But Zane surprised her, too. He was a lot better than he let on.

And when Zane's team won, there was a lot of ribbing that took place between Zane and Ben, who were on opposite teams.

"I was only trying to keep the kids safe," Ben said to Zane as they gathered for hot chocolate around a campfire, near the lake, after everyone had put away their hockey gear. "I didn't play like I could have."

"Right," Zane said with a knowing grin. "You just don't want to admit that I'm better than you."

"Now wait a minute," Ben said.

The family laughed as the cousins teased one another and Dad regaled them with stories from his glory days.

Megan and Rachel stood close to Liv while the children ran off to play in the snow. Dad, Ben, Charlie and Zane stood on the other side of the campfire, and Mom had gone into the lodge to get lunch on the table.

"How's it going?" Megan asked Liv.

"With what?"

"With Miley, of course."

Liv glanced at her daughter as she rolled

in the snow with her cousins, her heart light. "It's going really well, actually. Way better than I could have imagined."

"I've seen the way she's always trying to get you and Zane together," Rachel added. "How are things in that department?"

"With Zane?" Liv lowered her voice, not wanting him to hear them talking.

Megan turned so her back was to the fire and she gave Liv a sly smile. "I've been noticing a few things, myself. Lots of flirting, some private smiles…"

Heat warmed Liv's cheeks, and not just from the campfire.

Zane glanced up at her, and though she didn't think he could hear them from where he was standing, there was something in his gaze she could not deny. Was it awareness? Interest?

It couldn't be. They had flirted a little, but he'd given her no hint that he was interested in more. At least, that's what she kept telling herself.

"There's nothing to notice," Liv said, suddenly uncomfortable with the direction in conversation.

"I see how you two look at each other," Megan said with a girlish giggle. "How you sit close to each other and how you search for him when you enter a room."

Liv's stomach began to knot with doubt. Had she been that obvious? She hadn't meant to let her feelings show.

"What's wrong?" Rachel asked, searching Liv's face.

Megan's smile fell and she moved a little closer to Liv. "What's going on, Liv? Aren't you interested in Zane?"

It was Liv's turn to put her back to the fire and face the lake. She couldn't look at Zane or risk him seeing her reaction to this conversation. He was very perceptive of her feelings and if he thought something was off, he'd make a point to ask her about it later. She had no desire to discuss this with him. Now or later.

"I do care about Zane—more than I should," she said in a quiet voice to her sisters-in-law. "But I can't let myself love him."

"Why not?" Megan put her hand on Liv's arm. "You two were perfect together in high school, and you seem more perfect together now. The four of you could make an incredible family."

Each of Liv's failed relationships sprang to mind—each with one thing in common. Her.

"I don't want to ruin what we have—or

what they have." She swallowed the lump in her throat. "I wouldn't want to mess things up for anyone. What if we end up hurting each other—like I always end up doing in a relationship? I couldn't take that risk, not with Miley and Alexis involved. I'd rather just stay friends with Zane."

"Why would you hurt him?" Rachel asked.

"I've never had a successful relationship," Liv admitted, though Rachel should be well aware. "I'm incapable of loving people the way I should."

"That's ridiculous." Megan scoffed. "You love better than most people I know."

"I have a whole list of failed relationships to prove you wrong."

"A failed relationship doesn't prove you are incapable of love. Look at the way you love your nieces and nephews," Megan said. "And the way you love Miley and Alexis."

"Not to mention us or your brothers," Rachel added. "And your friend Piper. Liv, you are an amazing person with an incredible heart and a great capacity to love unconditionally."

"But those relationships you mentioned aren't romantic ones. I've messed up every relationship I've ever had with a boyfriend, starting with Zane."

"Then maybe that's your answer," Megan said softly. "Heal what broke between you and Zane and your capacity to love will be complete."

It sounded too good to be true—and too much to risk. What if it didn't work? What if she couldn't heal what had broken in her when she and Zane went their separate ways?

"Look at your relationship with Miley," Megan went on. "For the longest time, you thought you had been heartless to give her away. But the truth was, you didn't have a choice, so you hardened your heart, hoping it wouldn't hurt as much."

Liv glanced at Miley again, admitting to herself that Megan was speaking the truth.

"I always thought there was something broken in me that had allowed her to be taken from me." Liv's eyes filled with tears, but she didn't force them away. "What I've realized is that it broke *after* she was taken, not before."

"Which proves there's nothing wrong with you, Liv." Rachel put her hand on Liv's arm. "All of our hearts would break under those circumstances. But look at how much has healed in just under two weeks' time. Just think how much more could heal between you and Zane, if you'd let it."

Liv wiped at the single tear that cascaded

down her cold cheek. She wanted to believe it was possible, yet she wasn't sure if it would be worth the risk to find out. She could gain the greatest love of her life, but she could also lose the people she loved most in the world along the way.

Megan and Rachel turned back to face the fire, so Liv did, too.

Zane was looking at her when she glanced up, a question in his beautiful brown eyes. Compassion mingled with curiosity, so Liv braved a wobbly smile, hoping he wouldn't inquire.

But knowing he probably would.

Chapter Thirteen

Something was wrong, but Zane wasn't sure if he should ask Liv what was bothering her. The smile she had just offered him was a cover-up for the tears she wiped away, although she didn't give him any indication that she wanted to talk to him. Instead, she avoided his eye contact the second her smile disappeared.

"Lunchtime!" Marilyn called from the deck.

The kids began to run toward the lodge, but Zane wasn't ready to go inside. If something was bothering Liv, he wanted to help, if he could—especially if it concerned Miley.

As everyone moved away from the campfire, he tried to get close enough to Liv to ask her what was wrong. She kept up a conversation with Megan and Rachel the whole way, not once turning in his direction.

And back in the lodge, she didn't meet his gaze or sit near him as they ate.

He waited patiently, knowing that at some point she would be free to talk. After lunch was finished and cleaned up, everyone went up to the main room to play board games, but Liv didn't stay. She disappeared up the stairs and didn't come back.

Zane was about to go looking for her when Megan caught his eye.

"Is everything okay?" she asked him, joining him by the stairs while everyone was pulling out the board games.

"Do you know what happened to Liv?" He glanced up the stairs, but she was nowhere to be seen.

"I think she went to her room to rest for a bit."

Rest? Liv hadn't taken a single nap all week. She had more energy than most of the kids and had been in the midst of all of them every chance she could get.

"Is she okay?" His heart pounded a little harder, worried that something wasn't right.

Megan paused, as if weighing the wisdom in speaking. "She's just a little overwhelmed right now."

"With what? Miley?"

"Well," Megan said carefully, "there's a lot

on her heart right now, and she's still uncertain of the future."

He had tried easing her burdens and answering her questions. The last thing he wanted was for her to feel unsure. "Is it something I did?"

"No." Megan shook her head. "It's nothing like that."

Yet, he couldn't shake the feeling that it *did* have something to do with him. Things had been going so well with her and Miley this past week, he was almost certain she wasn't questioning motherhood.

"She's just sorting some things out." Megan smiled. "I have a feeling it will all work out in the end, though."

What did that mean?

Megan patted his arm and gave him a meaningful look. "She's more confused than anything." And, with that, she left his side to join the children.

Confused? About him? Had he come on too strong this past week? He had tried hiding his feelings for her, while looking for any indication that she might return his affection, yet she hadn't given him any hint, other than a little flirting now and then. Until he knew for sure, one way or the other, he wasn't prepared to bare his heart.

But he wasn't ready to let her go without trying. He had made a point to have alone time with her in the mornings, hoping they would get a chance to open up about their feelings toward one another. Whenever he ventured into those waters, she ended up changing the subject. She made a point to talk about the resort, answering his questions for the article he was writing. They also discussed his plans to move to Timber Falls, and she answered all his questions about the schools, the community and her church. She told him about her friends and her work. He had loved getting to know her better, yet they hadn't once spoken about what he really wanted to discuss.

Either she was completely oblivious, or she was deliberately ignoring the subject. Unfortunately, he was afraid the latter was true.

"Daddy," Miley called out to him. "Do you want to play?"

"Maybe later." He didn't think he could concentrate enough to play a board game right now.

Miley left her cousins and came up to him. "What's wrong?" she asked.

She was a perceptive little girl, which he usually applauded, but right now he wasn't ready to share his troubles with her.

"Nothing's wrong. Why don't you go back to the game?"

"Is there something wrong with Liv?" She studied him. "Where did she go?"

"You don't need to worry about the grown-ups, Miley." He put his hand on the top of her head.

Miley took his hand and then led him to the corner of the main room, away from everyone else. There were a few leather chairs there, near a big window, with a stack of magazines on a coffee table. Miley tugged Zane to sit on one of the chairs, and she took the other one.

"Is this about me?" she asked him.

He couldn't hide his surprise. "You? Why would this be about you?"

"Do you like Liv, Daddy?"

"Of course I like Liv. But what does that have to do with you?"

"Does she like you?"

"I believe she does."

"Do you want to marry her?"

"Miley—"

"She said you loved each other before. Why don't you marry her?"

"It's not that easy."

"Because of me?"

He frowned and put his hand on her shoulder. "Why do you keep saying that?"

"Kendra told me her mom and dad were talking about you and Liv."

"Sweetie, you shouldn't listen to what other people say—"

"Kendra said Auntie Rachel was telling Uncle Charlie that Liv won't date you because of me."

Zane's stomach turned at Miley's words. He was frustrated that they were talking about them, but he was also hurt that Liv wasn't interested in pursuing a relationship—confirming what he had suspected all week. Anger threatened to rise up within him, and he glanced across the room to where Rachel was sitting next to Alexis. He didn't appreciate them gossiping in front of their children, but maybe they didn't know Kendra was listening. And, if he was honest with himself, he had already suspected they were discussing his life. It would be strange if they didn't care enough to talk about it. They loved Liv and they were concerned about her.

"Is it true?" Miley asked Zane.

"I don't know." He lowered his hand and leaned back in his chair. "But you don't need to worry about any of this."

"But I want Liv to date you."

He stared at his daughter. "Even after learning the truth about what happened when we were teenagers?"

Miley shrugged. "Why not?"

Zane didn't have an answer.

"If she won't date you because of me," Miley said, imploring him with her eyes, "can I tell her I want her to?"

"No." He shook his head, alarmed at the thought of Miley taking this up with Liv but more alarmed to think that maybe she already had. "You didn't talk to Liv about this already, did you?" That might explain why she had become so standoffish toward him.

"No."

"Good. I don't want you to talk to Liv about dating me. This is a grown-up issue and we are able to talk about it without you."

"So, you'll tell her?" Miley sat up straight, her face filled with hope and excitement.

What could he say that would pacify her but wouldn't give her false hope? "You need to let Liv and I talk about this. Do you understand?"

"Will you tell her I want her to marry you?"

"Miley, I've already told you. There are too many obstacles between us. I really don't think it's realistic to hope for such a thing."

"But if she marries you, she can be my real mom."

He tilted his head. "Baby, she already is your real mom."

"But she could live with us and she could be Alexis's mom, too."

Zane didn't know what else to say to his daughter, so he just offered a sad smile and then nodded at her cousins. "Go back to your games and let me worry about all this."

Miley finally stood, but before she walked away, she asked again, "Will you tell her?"

"I don't know." It was the truth. If Liv had no interest in dating him, he wouldn't risk hurting or embarrassing her by bringing it up. It was better if they let things lie. They already had enough to worry about with all the transitions they were about to make.

As Miley walked back to her cousins, she turned once, a disappointed frown marring her face, but he waved her on and gave her a smile, hoping to brighten her mood.

The truth was, he wanted to see Liv again—wanted more time alone with her. They would soon be leaving and then they'd be busy getting on with their lives.

He suddenly realized that in the chaos of their week, she hadn't finished the tour of the resort. He needed to take a few more pictures, and he wanted to see inside some of the cabins near the lake. It might have been easier to ask Marilyn or Bob to take him—or to even go by himself—but he wanted the pleasure of her company.

And maybe, just maybe, if she gave him any inkling that she was interested, he could finally tell her what he had wanted to say all week.

He wanted more of Liv in his life—as much as she'd give him.

But first, he needed to convince her to take him on another tour.

Soft snowflakes brushed against the window outside Liv's suite. They were delicate and gentle, and if Liv didn't know there was a blizzard expected to start around midnight, she would have never imagined these small, lovely flakes could be a precursor to a violent storm. The weatherman had forecasted up to seven inches of snow and winds gusting to over fifty miles an hour.

Liv stood near the window, her arms wrapped around herself, thinking over the past week since they had told Miley the truth. Something wonderful had begun and was unfolding each day. With Miley's newfound knowledge and Liv's ability to be open with her, they had experienced many special moments together. Now when she shared a family tradition, it was with the full understanding of Miley's connection to those things. And Liv was happier than she dreamed possible, yet her spirit was still heavy. Was this week just a precursor to an oncoming storm?

When Megan and Rachel had broached the subject of her feelings toward Zane, she hadn't been ready to voice her fears, but they had given her no choice. Now alone in her room, she had to face the truth. She was afraid to open her heart to Zane, not only because she was fearful of hurting him, but she was scared to hurt any chance she might have at being a part of Miley's life. If something went wrong between her and Zane, then how would that affect her relationship with Miley and Alexis?

No matter the cost, she would have to suppress her feelings and not allow herself to fall in love with Zane again. It was that simple.

At least, she wished it could be that simple. It was one thing to tell her head to cooperate and another to tell her heart.

A knock at her door caused Liv to turn away from the window. No doubt one of the nieces or nephews had come up to get her. They loved spending time with her as much as she did with them, and they were often at her door for one reason or another.

But when she opened the door, it was Zane standing in the hallway, alone.

Her heart did a little flip at the unexpected sight of him.

His hair was a bit disheveled, and he'd neglected to shave again, but maturity and age had been kind to him and made him more masculine and handsome than before. Yet it was his dark eyes, and the way he looked at her, that made her pulse skitter with awareness.

She should have known he would come looking for her after what had happened at the campfire. She had tried to avoid him at lunch, but he wasn't so easily swayed off course. It was both comforting and a little annoying that he was persistent and could read her so well.

He leaned against her doorframe, his hands in his pockets. "How are you doing?"

It was disconcerting to have him standing there, so at ease when her insides felt like a swirling blizzard. If he knew the torment she was facing concerning her feelings toward him, would he be so chill?

Or would he be appalled?

The truth was, she had no idea how he even felt about her. He had been attentive, and had flirted with her over the past week, but that was Zane. He was the kind of man who was thoughtful and attentive to everyone. If there was a smile to be had, Zane was usually the one to bring it about. He loved to make people laugh and feel good, so maybe that was all he was doing with her. Perhaps all of this inner turmoil was for naught, since he probably had no interest in pursuing a relationship beyond partnering to raise Miley together. She was worrying for nothing. Why couldn't she simply enjoy his company and be content as friends? That would save her a lot of heartache in the long run.

"I'm doing well," she said, truly feeling it for the first time in a while.

"Good." He smiled and it nearly undid her resolve to rein in her heart. "I was wondering if you could give me one last tour. I haven't seen the cabins by the lake and I'd like to get a few shots of the lodge from near the water. We don't have much time left before it's dark and with the storm coming in, I might not have time to get the pictures tomorrow."

"Of course I can take you." It would give her a good excuse to get out of the lodge and stretch her legs a bit. She loved her family, and enjoyed the kids, but it would be nice to get a little time away from it all. "I'll be ready to go as soon as I get changed."

"Okay." He didn't move away to get ready but stayed right where he was, watching her. He looked like he wanted to say something more but hesitated.

"What?" She smiled at him, waiting for him to tell her what was on his mind.

"Nothing." He finally pushed away from the door. "It can wait."

She hated waiting, and he knew that. He used to tease her about being impatient in high school. "What did you want to say?" She walked into the hall as he went to his suite.

"It can wait," he said again with a chuckle.

"Zane Harris!"

"I still know how to get under your skin, don't I?" With that, he entered his suite and closed the door.

Liv couldn't help but laugh. She loved feeling lighthearted with Zane and his teasing just confirmed her earlier revelation. Zane enjoyed making people happy and he would feel especially obligated to make her smile, given the difficulty they'd been through.

Life had been too serious. It was good to laugh again, and she had Zane to thank for that.

They met a few minutes later, dressed for outside, and left the lodge, telling the adults where they were going.

Zane brought his camera, but it wouldn't be light out for long. The sky was getting darker by the minute with heavy clouds pushing in from the west.

"We won't have much time," Liv said, "before it's too dark to get your pictures."

Snow continued to fall, in large thick flakes now, giving the resort a snow-globe effect. It was breathtaking.

"Let's stop here so I can snap some pictures of the lodge." Zane pulled out his camera, and though Liv wasn't much of a photographer, she could admire the quality.

"I bet you've taken some amazing pictures all over the world." She watched him set up his shot, adjusting a few buttons on the camera, before taking the picture.

He looked at the images on the display screen before changing the settings again. He had taken a photography class in high school and she remembered spending hours with him, traipsing through downtown Marshall to take pictures. Among the live-action scenes and the still life, he had taken several photos of her. It had been a lovely fall day, just a couple weeks before she had gotten pregnant.

Liv waited for the pang of regret to sting at the thought of her pregnancy, yet it didn't come. For the first time in eleven years, the thought of that time in her life didn't hold the same remorse and guilt. With the truth out in the open, and the forgiveness Miley had offered, there was no more heaviness in Liv's heart.

Instead, something light and almost exciting filled her at the thought of that memory. Was it possible to look back and be glad again? A smile lifted her lips as the realization dawned.

Zane watched her for a moment and then he turned his camera on her.

Embarrassment warmed her cheeks. "What are you doing?"

"You look so pretty, standing in the snow, with that smile on your face." He snapped another picture and lowered the camera. "I haven't seen you look this happy in a long time." He paused for a second. "*Are* you happy, Liv?"

She was happy. And it was such a foreign concept, it took her a moment to identify the feeling. "I am."

"It makes me happy to know you're happy." He showed her the photo he had taken. "Look how beautiful you are."

Liv studied the shot, another wave of embarrassment filling her cheeks with heat. She did look pretty—but she felt silly saying so—yet the embarrassment was also due to his compliment.

"What do you see when you look at your picture?" he asked.

She couldn't help but notice the wrinkles just starting to form around her eyes, but she wouldn't tell Zane she saw age in the picture. "I see a woman with a lot of life behind her."

"That's funny," he said as he studied the picture. "Because I see a woman with a lot of life ahead of her." His gaze returned to her face and his eyes softened. "The best is yet to come, Liv."

Was it possible? "I hope you're right."

He put the camera strap over his shoulder and took a step closer to her. There was nothing but snow and lake and resort all around them. No people, no distractions, nothing needing their attention.

"I hope I can be part of the best that's yet to come." Zane's statement was full of meaning, yet Liv didn't want to assume.

Her pulse ticked in her wrists and a strange and wonderful feeling pooled in her stomach. He was so close she could smell the cologne he wore and see the golden specks in his brown eyes. Was he offering her what she thought? A chance to rekindle their relationship and look to the future together? She had never wanted him to kiss her as much as she did in this moment, but a niggle of doubt pricked her conscience. Nothing had changed. He was still Miley's dad and if she did something to hurt her relationship with him, it would affect her relationship with Miley. It was too soon—and too tender—to risk such a thing.

Liv took a step back, needing some space and distance between her and Zane. She couldn't think straight when he was standing so close. All of her senses were overwhelmed, and her feelings for him were far stronger than her rational mind.

"We need to get to the cabins before it gets dark." She turned and started to walk down the path leading to the lake and the cabins along the shoreline.

Her pulse was erratic and her breathing was labored. She tried not to stumble over the uneven path and didn't know if Zane followed her because she didn't have the courage to turn around and meet his gaze. She couldn't risk letting her emotions get the better of her. She might say or do something to jeopardize what they already had, which was a good friendship. A very good friendship.

When she finally arrived at the cabins, she

stopped and waited for him to join her. She had brought a master key to open each door, but she wasn't sure if she wanted to take him inside. The cabins were intimate and cozy— the opposite of what she wanted with Zane right now.

"My mom is planning a special supper for our New Year's Eve celebration," Liv said to Zane without meeting his gaze. "I should probably get back to help her."

"Did I say something back there to offend you?"

"No. Of course not." She fumbled with the key and put it in the door, trying to make her voice sound light. "All of the cabins are basically cookie cutters of each other, so if you've seen one, you've seen them all." She finally got the door unlocked and pushed it open. "I'll let you go in and take a look around. You probably want to get some pictures, so I won't come in to bother you. I'll wait out here."

"Liv." Zane didn't enter the cabin, but stood near her and the open door. "What's wrong?"

"Nothing." She couldn't tell him what was bothering her because she didn't want to have that conversation. It was easier not dealing with the issue, wasn't it? She didn't want to reject him, so if she didn't let him talk to her about their relationship, she wouldn't have to.

He stood there for a moment, but she refused to meet his gaze. He eventually sighed and went inside.

She closed the door and waited for him on the little porch connected to the cabin. The water was only a stone's throw away. It was frozen and covered in snow, but it was still peaceful in its quiet desolation. The air was bitter cold, and her breath fogged around her mouth. It would have been warmer in the cabin, but she didn't want to put herself in a position she would regret with Zane.

After a few minutes, he came back outside.

"Did you get what you wanted?"

"No." He shook his head, his voice heavy. "But I guess I have what I need and that has to be good enough."

Liv frowned, but he didn't bother to clarify. Instead, he waited for her to lock up the cabin, and then they started back toward the lodge.

The sun had fallen on the last day of the year, and as much as Liv wanted to believe the year ahead would be the best of her life, she wasn't sure.

Zane's flirting had changed, and the truth was, she couldn't pass it off as him simply being kind and thoughtful anymore. A man with platonic feelings wouldn't be showering her with so much attention or want to spend as much time with her. Things had definitely changed and she wasn't sure how to proceed.

Chapter Fourteen

Laughter filled the air as the family gathered around the fireplace in the main room of the lodge. Zane sat on one of the couches, trying to stay involved in the game of fishbowl they were playing, yet he was easily distracted by Liv, who sat on the opposite side of the room.

It was only fifteen minutes to midnight and all of the children had been allowed to stay awake until the New Year. The five-year-olds, Alexis, Jackson and Anders, had tried to stay awake, but each one had fallen asleep over the past hour and been brought to their bed. It was only the four older kids and the adults left to play fishbowl, the game Zane had learned since arriving at the lodge.

Each person was given three slips of paper, on which they could write any person, place or thing. When all the papers were put into the fishbowl, the group was divided into two teams and a minute timer was set. For the first round, one team member would pull papers out of the bowl and try to get his or her team to guess what was on the paper by giving several clues. That team member would keep going until the timer ran out and then it was the next team's turn. When all the papers were guessed, they went back into the fishbowl and the second round started. The papers were then acted out by team members with a timer. The third round, only a one-word clue was given for each paper. At the end of the third round, all the correct guesses were added up and the team with the highest points won.

The game had been fun, and they had played it several times over the past week, but tonight, Zane couldn't get excited. His visit to the cabin with Liv had left him feeling flat and disappointed—more than disappointed. He had given her the opportunity to open up about the future, but she had shut down the conversation. If he had been confused and uncertain about her feelings before, he wasn't now.

The game came to an end and Miley's team won. Zane smiled at his daughter's excitement, but when they suggested another game, he opted out. He wasn't in the mood to keep playing, and he knew he would only drag down everyone else's enthusiasm if he tried.

"Only five minutes until midnight," Bob told the kids. "Let's put away the games for the night and I'll set a countdown timer."

"Who wants to help me pour the sparkling juice?" Marilyn asked.

The kids eagerly went off with Grammy to her private kitchen. Bob followed, fidgeting with his phone timer as he went.

Ben and Megan sat together on a love seat with Liv. It looked crowded, but no one seemed to mind. Charlie sat in an easy chair, giving Rachel a back rub as she sat on the ground in front of him. And Zane was on a large couch all by himself.

Megan and Rachel had glanced between Zane and Liv all evening, questions in their eyes. Even Ben had shot his sister a curious look when she had pushed her way onto the love seat with him and Megan.

But Liv had not once looked in Zane's direction. She was definitely avoiding him.

This was a great way to end the year and start a new one.

While Megan, Ben, Rachel and Charlie talked about people they knew in Marshall,

Liv and Zane didn't say a word. More than anything, he wished she would come sit next to him. He wanted to tell her that if she didn't want to talk about the future, they didn't need to. He didn't want to lose their comradery and friendship, especially now, when they had just found each other again.

He looked at her, hoping she would glance in his direction. Even though he didn't have anything he needed to apologize for, he did want to smooth things over. But he wasn't sure if she'd be willing to talk. She would probably be too afraid he'd want to confront her again.

Embarrassment warmed his neck just thinking about the way she had shut down his statement earlier. She hadn't rejected him—not really—but if he had pressed, maybe she would have. He wouldn't take the risk again. So maybe it was better if he didn't try to smooth things over. Maybe he should also pretend it didn't happen.

Liv glanced at her phone and sighed.

"What's wrong?" Megan asked her.

"It just feels like this last five minutes is taking forever." Liv glanced up at Megan and offered a smile that didn't quite reach her eyes. "I'm tired."

"I think we all are," Rachel said. "We'll need to go home and rest from our vacation."

Megan reached over and gave Liv a side hug.

Zane tried not to notice the change in mood. This past week had been fun and carefree, but something had shifted today and he was smart enough to know it had to do with him. He had pressed Liv too far and now everyone was feeling the weight of it.

If the storm wasn't blowing in, he would pack up his girls and head out in the morning. The house he planned to rent in Timber Falls was ready for him and the girls to move into on the first of January. Since he had no furniture or household goods, it would take a while to purchase everything he needed, but it would give him something to occupy his mind. He had the article to write, since it was due on the tenth, and the girls would start school on the third.

He just needed to get through one more day at Lakepoint Lodge before he could bury himself in the busyness of getting his family settled.

The only trouble was, Liv would be there to help. No doubt she would offer to keep the girls overnight at her house until he could get them some beds, and she would probably offer to feed them until he could stock his kitchen. She had already volunteered to take them shopping for school supplies and clothes as soon as they got to Timber Falls.

There was no getting away from Liv now, and while that pleased him, it also felt like torture. How would he see her every day and keep his heart in check? The more time he spent with her, the more he longed for her. It was only getting worse and seeing how upset he had made her just added to the torment.

"Just another minute," Bob said as he led the way back into the main room with Marilyn and the four older children in tow.

As Marilyn handed out the glasses of sparkling juice, all the adults got to their feet for the countdown.

The lights on the Christmas tree twinkled and the excitement from the children filled the room.

Liv stayed on one side of the mass of people and Zane on the other.

"Get ready," Bob called out to everyone. "Five…four…three…two…one! Happy New Year!"

Bob's phone began to play "Auld Lang Syne" as everyone cheered and toasted the New Year. When the glasses were put down, the kisses began, first with Bob and Marilyn, and then with Ben and Megan and Charlie and Rachel.

Zane gave Miley a big hug. "Happy New Year, sweetie."

"Happy New Year, Daddy." She kissed his cheek and then giggled before she went on to wish the next person a happy New Year.

He watched her surrounded by her new family, thanking God for bringing her to their inner circle.

"Happy New Year, Zane," Bob said, extending his hand for a shake. "I'm looking forward to what this year will bring to you and your family."

"I am, too." It would bring a lot of changes—that was for sure.

"Happy New Year." Megan gave Zane a big hug, squeezing him hard in her exuberance.

"Happy New Year." He returned the hug, noticing that he and Liv were moving closer together as everyone extended well wishes for the upcoming year.

When she turned, and found herself facing Zane, she paused.

Everything except Liv faded from Zane's senses. She was so lovely with her hair unbound and flowing around her shoulders. Even though she was dressed in a simple sweater and jeans, she looked amazing. The color was high in her cheeks, causing her blue eyes to sparkle.

They stood there for a moment, neither one speaking, and then she came into his arms and he hugged her tight, closing his eyes to shut out everything but her.

"Happy New Year, Zane," she whispered.

"Happy New Year, Liv." He didn't want to let her go.

She pulled back and her eyes dropped to his lips for a brief moment, yet it was long enough for Zane's heart rate to escalate and his pulse to beat erratically. He wanted to kiss her—more than anything—and now would be the time. New Year's was made for kissing, wasn't it?

But he wouldn't kiss her here, in front of everyone, and he definitely wouldn't kiss her without her permission.

He was about to let her go, but she came close to him again and placed a gentle kiss on his cheek. "I'm sorry," she whispered and then she pulled away and was on the other side of the room again before he could stop her and ask what she meant.

"I think it's time for bed," Rachel said, taking Kendra's and Leah's hands into her own. "Good night, everyone. Sweet dreams."

"Good night," they all responded.

Megan and Ben led the way up the stairs with Nicole, leaving Miley behind. She yawned and started toward the stairs, apparently not concerned about whether Zane was coming up to their suite with her.

"Do you need any help?" he asked his daughter.

She turned and gave him a look she had been perfecting for a while. It was the one that told him she was far too old to be babied. "I know how to brush my own teeth and find my pajamas, Daddy."

Zane put up his hands. "Okay. I'll be up in a while to pray for you."

Miley started toward the stairs again, but she paused and turned around, then she ran across the short space and wrapped her arms around Liv. "I forgot to wish you a happy New Year."

Liv's smile was bright and surprised. She hugged Miley and placed a kiss on the top of her head. "Happy New Year."

Apparently satisfied, Miley let go of Liv and ran back toward the stairs.

"It's shocking how much energy she still has at this hour." Marilyn laughed as she started to clean up the dishes scattered about the room.

Liv began to help, but Marilyn waved her aside. "Go to bed, Olivia. You look tired."

"You and Dad shouldn't have to clean up by yourselves." Liv picked up the papers from fishbowl and tossed them into the garbage can.

Zane wasn't tired, at least, not anymore. Not since Liv's kiss and her strange apology. Why was she sorry? What had she done? He wanted to talk to her, but would she let him?

He started to help clean, too.

"No, you don't," Bob said to Zane. "You're our guest. You don't need to clean."

"That's just nonsense," Zane said to his host. "You shouldn't have to do all the work."

"I'm serious," Bob said. "Go on up to bed."

"I'm not tired."

"Then go outside and check on the weather. See if that blizzard has started." Bob laughed, but Zane didn't think it was a bad idea.

"Mind if I light the fire table out there?" He really wasn't tired and could use some time to think.

"Be my guest." Bob continued to clean and moved away from Zane.

Zane glanced at Liv, hoping she'd ask to join him, but she left the room with a tray of glasses, without looking back.

* * *

The lodge was quiet and the ticking clock in Mom and Dad's living room sounded louder than usual as Liv filled the dishwasher with the glasses. It was just a few minutes past midnight, but the year felt old to Liv already. Instead of feeling like she was getting a fresh start, she realized that she was still carrying around a lot of baggage she'd been dealing with for years. It would be so much easier if she could just choose to let it go and then move on with her life. Yet, it wasn't that easy. Some wounds took longer to heal than others.

Mom entered the kitchen and set down the large bowls that had been full of popcorn earlier. "Zane is heading out to the deck."

"I know. I heard him talking to Dad."

"Are you going to join him?"

Liv didn't turn away from her task to look at her mom. Instead, she continued to load the dishwasher and simply shook her head.

The door opened and Dad entered. He held the fishbowl in his hands and set it down on the counter. "That Zane is a good kid."

"He's not a kid, Dad."

"You know what I mean." Dad pulled out a stool from the counter and took a seat. "I like him."

"Good. I'm glad."

Mom stood next to Dad and leaned against the counter. "I definitely think we misjudged him."

Liv stopped loading the dishwasher and turned to face her parents, a glass in hand. "What?"

"All these years, I thought he was a selfish, reckless kid." Mom shrugged. "I was wrong."

It took every shred of willpower Liv possessed not to lose her patience with her mom. "I tried telling you that eleven years ago, but you wouldn't listen."

"Olivia," Mom said with a sigh. "When Miley is seventeen, you and I will talk again about what it's like to parent a teenager. Until then, please give me the benefit of the doubt when it comes to things like this. It's not easy being objective when your teenage daughter comes to you with an unplanned pregnancy."

Liv let out a breath of frustration and nodded. It would be hard to understand where her mother was coming from until she lived through her experience, which Liv hoped would never happen.

"He's a great father," Dad went on to say, "and an amazing writer. I've read some of his articles online."

"He's also a hard worker and a great outdoorsman." Mom put her chin in her hand.

"And, he loves Jesus, so he ticks off all the boxes on my list."

"He can play hockey, too," Dad added, as if that was somewhere high on this imaginary list.

"All the boxes?" Liv set the glass down and crossed her arms. "What are you two talking about?"

"We've seen what's been happening between the two of you," Mom said. "And we want you to know that you have our blessing. We think he's perfect for you."

"Wait." Liv held up her hands. "Mom, you just told me last week that Zane and I didn't deserve a happily-ever-after and that it would only complicate matters if we dated. That we should put Miley first."

Mom shrugged. "That was last week. I've changed my mind."

"You can't change your mind." Indignation rose up in Liv's chest.

"Why not?" Mom frowned. "Isn't that what you wanted me to say? That I like Zane, that I was wrong all this time and you two are perfect for each other? That I think you and Zane are an amazing team and you would be better together than apart? Why can't I say that, when I realize I've been wrong this whole time?"

Liv put her hands up to cover her face, her frustration coming out in a moan. Her mother's roller-coaster personality was driving her to distraction.

"What about forfeiting our happily-ever-after?" Liv asked, pulling her hands down to stare at her mom. "We made a mistake and now we will have to pay for that mistake."

"How long do you think you should pay?" Dad asked quietly, watching Liv through his sad eyes. "Because I think you have repaid any perceived debt you incurred and then some." His voice grew even gentler. "Liv, Jesus paid the price for our sins. Yes, sometimes there are consequences to those decisions, and you know that full well. But Jesus forgave you. It's time to forgive yourself and move on. You paid the consequences. You missed out on the first eleven years of Miley's life, and you missed out on a relationship with Zane. But God has brought them back into your life and you no longer have to miss out. You have the choice to be a part of their lives. Don't continue to inflict punishment upon yourself that you don't deserve. It would be a shame if you did."

Liv studied her dad, his words like a bandage, binding up her fractured soul. "But what if I fail? What if our relationship is a disaster? I'll ruin any chance I have of being close to Miley."

"No, you won't." Mom frowned. "First, you and Zane are incredible together. If anyone has a chance at true happiness it's you two. You've already weathered a devastating storm and come out on the other side together. If that's not a testament to the staying power of your relationship, I don't know what is."

"And, the truth is, Liv," Dad went on, "every relationship is rocky. Every single one has mountains and valleys. You will struggle, you will fight, you will not always see eye to eye, but when you're committed, and you have children, and the stakes are higher, so too is the devotion and sacrifice you're willing to make. Miley and Alexis will both be better off watching you love each other, through the good and the bad, reaffirming your commitment to each other and to your family, than they will watching you live two separate lives."

"Your dad and I haven't always been as strong as we are," Mom said as she straightened and came around the counter to face Liv. "I know I aggravate him and I know he hates when I lose my temper and say things I regret."

Dad made a face, as if indicating she was making an understatement.

"But he's right there beside me, usually behind closed doors, speaking truth and love to me. It's because of your father that I can finally see the truth about my part in your unhappiness. And it's because of his love for me that I believe in your love for Zane."

What Mom was saying was true. Liv had witnessed it a hundred times throughout her life. Her dad was her mother's rock and support. He was there to cheer her on and to hold her accountable. They worked well as a team, but it didn't mean they were always in agreement or that they didn't fight.

"I think the difference between Zane and all the other men you've dated over the years," Dad said, "is that you weren't willing to make sacrifices for them or the relationships they had to offer. Zane is different, because he's the one."

The truth was so startling, and so clear, Liv's eyes filled with tears.

Zane *was* the one. He had always been the one. She could have made the other relationships work, but she hadn't wanted to, because they weren't Zane. She wasn't broken as much as she was wounded. And wounds were not permanent.

"There's a young man out there, waiting on the deck," Dad said, "who is ready and willing to offer you his heart. I can see it in his eyes. And I think the greatest gift you can offer him and his girls is taking the risk to offer yours in return."

Liv could no longer control the tears. They streamed down her face as she walked around the counter and wrapped her arms around her dad in a big hug.

He returned the hug, holding her close. "I love you, Liv."

"I love you, too, Dad."

Mom was standing in line for her hug, which Liv easily gave to her.

"I'm sorry for my part in your pain," Mom whispered, her voice broken with tears. "Please don't let the next eleven years pass you by without reaching for the things you want."

"I won't." Not if she could help it.

Liv smiled and wiped away her tears, her heart beating hard and true for the first time in a long time. "Do you mind finishing the dishes?"

Mom and Dad laughed as they wiped their tears away.

"Go," Mom said. "And grab ahold of some happiness."

Liv didn't wait for her to say it again, but left the kitchen and headed toward the deck.

Chapter Fifteen

The sky over Lake Madeline was pitch-black and the only light Zane had to see the snow was from the fire table. Thankfully the wind hadn't picked up, yet, but the snow was falling steadily, almost like rain. When it hit the flames, it disintegrated and melted all around the fire table.

Zane was warm, sitting in his coat and hat, yet he wasn't comfortable. A restlessness had been building up within him and it was so overpowering, he was tempted to go on a run. If it wasn't supposed to start storming in earnest within the hour, he might have taken off for a bit to release the tension.

His heart was heavy with longing for Liv and with disappointment that she didn't return his feelings. If he was honest with himself, he'd never stopped loving her, though the affection and regard he felt for her had gone dormant while he'd been married to Tanya. He could never fully forget Liv. Miley's presence in his life had kept his love for Liv alive in his heart, whether he had wanted it to or not. If it wasn't her eyes or her blond hair that reminded him of Liv, it was her mannerisms and the way she carried herself.

And the truth was, all his love needed to resprout and grow had been seeing Liv again. He loved her, had always loved her and would always love her. The thought of that love going unanswered for the rest of his life felt like a burden he was not prepared to carry.

The door opened and Liv appeared.

Zane's heart skipped a beat at the sight of her. Her eyes were glistening in the reflection from the flames as she met his gaze.

In that moment, Zane knew he would love no other woman the way he loved Liv Butler. It was impossible. She had been his first love and his true love, and though he loved Tanya and had been faithful to her, he was smart enough to know the difference.

"Mind if I join you?" she asked in a hushed tone.

He shook his head, not trusting his voice.

She closed the door behind her, just as the

remaining lights inside Lakepoint Lodge flipped off.

It was completely dark now, except for the light of the flames. Thick snow fell, collecting on their heads and shoulders, on the tree branches next to the lodge and on the floor of the deck.

Zane stood when she reached the fire table, wondering what she was doing outside. Had she come to tell him why she was sorry? Or to confront him about his statements earlier and about the way he had come on too strong this week?

She stopped near the fire table, close to him.

He didn't move—didn't breathe—afraid he would say something he'd regret.

A gust of wind whipped around the lodge, causing the flames to dance and pushing Liv a little closer to Zane.

"It looks like the blizzard is about to start," she said quietly.

"It's getting colder by the second," he replied, though he wanted to say a dozen different things.

"Do you like storms?"

He studied her face, questions swirling through his mind. "I like them when I can be inside and watch them from the safety of a warm home—or here, by the fire."

"Me, too. Stormy weather is my favorite."

Another gust of wind blew against them and this time, Zane moved around Liv to block her from the brunt of it. He stood very close to her, feeling both protective and ready to face whatever storm came their way together.

Liv didn't move away from him, and if he wasn't mistaken, she stepped even closer.

She was so close, he could no longer see her face.

"Zane?"

"Yes?"

"I'm sorry."

There it was again, the apology. He had to look at her face—had to see into her eyes to understand what she was trying to say to him.

He pulled back and she looked up at him.

"Sorry for what, Liv?"

"For how blind I've been."

"How blind? To what?"

"To you."

His heart started to beat hard and the thought of the cold and the wind disappeared, yet he couldn't speak.

"You told me down by the lake that you wanted to be a part of the best that's yet to come." She swallowed as she studied him in the flickering light, uncertainty and apprehension in her gaze. "What did you mean by that?"

It was his turn to swallow hard. Fear tightened his throat. What if he told her the truth and she rejected him? Was she ready to hear what he had to say? There was no way to find out unless he said what was on his heart.

"I want to offer you my future, Liv." His voice was thick with emotion and the love he felt for her. "I want to share a life with you. I want to raise the girls with you. I want you by my side through the good and the bad and the best that's yet to come."

Tears gathered in her eyes as a gentle smile lit up her face.

"I love you, Liv Butler." He could hardly believe that after all this time, he was facing her, sharing his heart. Years of memories, both with her and without her, seemed to culminate in that moment. Everything had worked together to come to this time and place and he was ready to be honest and open. "I'm deeply in love with you. You're not only the mother of my first child, you're a dear friend and a person I have always admired. Your strength of character and your boundless energy leave me in awe. I know I don't deserve your love, but I want it, more than anything I've ever wanted before."

She lifted her arms to encircle the back of his neck, rising on her tiptoes, and right before she placed a kiss against his lips, she said, "You've always had it."

Her kiss was so tender and sweet, it undid every bit of reserve Zane possessed. He wrapped his arms around Liv and lifted her off her feet to meet her kiss with all the passion he'd ever felt for her. His kiss was deep and long, erasing years of heartache and replacing it with hope. He kissed her for what they had lost and for what they were about to gain. He found himself kissing her cheeks and chin and even the tip of her nose. He couldn't get enough of her.

They were both breathless when he finally set her on her feet again, but he didn't let her go—didn't think he could let her go anytime soon.

"I love you, Zane," she said as she smiled and wiped the melting snowflakes off her cheeks, or were those tears? "I've been so afraid to admit the truth to myself, but I can't deny it any longer. I've always loved you. I know I don't deserve your love, either, but I think that's what makes you and me the perfect match. Neither of us will ever deserve the love God has so lavishly allowed to grow in our hearts."

Zane was speechless with the awe and wonder of this love they shared. It hadn't come easily, but it was deep and rich and full of promise.

They stood in each other's arms for a long time, neither one seeming to be in any hurry to get out of the cold. Zane marveled at how much had changed between them while so much had remained the same.

"What are we going to do about our little problem?" he asked her playfully, after kissing her again.

"What problem?"

"The one that puts you in one house and me in the other?" He nuzzled her neck with his nose as he inhaled her scent and reveled in the softness of her skin. "There's been too much time and distance between us. I don't want to waste another day away from you."

She was nestled in his embrace, where she fit perfectly, her voice a little muffled from his coat. "Zane?"

"Yes?"

"What about Miley?" Her body seemed to tighten in his hold and he pulled back to look at her.

"What about Miley?"

"What will she think about all this?"

"She's going to be delighted."

Liv pulled back. "Are you sure?"

"I'm positive." He smiled. "Just this afternoon she told me to tell you that she wants you to date me."

A smile transformed Liv's worried face. "She does?"

"Yes. And I know Alexis would love it, too."

"Really?"

Zane let his smile drop. "But I don't want to date you, Liv."

Her smile disappeared, as well. "You don't?"

"I want to marry you."

The smile returned, with a little bit of shyness. "You do?"

"I do."

"Are you asking me to marry you, Zane?"

He had never imagined this moment would happen. It was something only God could have orchestrated and brought to pass. But Zane got down on one knee, in the falling snow, with the fire blowing in the wind, a blizzard descending upon them, and took Liv's hand in his own. "I don't have a ring, or even a set of kitchen utensils for that matter, but what I do have will outlast all of those things. I only have my heart—and my daughters—to offer to you today. But if you'll marry me, Liv, I'll have you, and I won't need anything else for as long as I live."

"Of course I'll marry you." She pulled him to his feet and wrapped her arms around him again. She met his eager lips with hers.

Zane's chest filled with warmth and it extended out into all his limbs. It didn't matter that the temperature had dropped below zero, or that the wind was whipping around the lodge with relentless energy or that the snow was piling up around them. He had never felt more comfortable or content in his life.

The moment Liv opened her eyes on New Year's morning, a smile spread over her face. She was warm and cozy, tucked under the covers of her large bed, while the blizzard continued to blow just outside the windows of her suite. The wind whipped about the eaves of the lodge with a ferociousness that would silence any wild animal, yet Liv was safe and secure in the log-framed building. It was quiet and tranquil in her room, like the peace she felt inside her heart. The world might be loud and dangerous, but everything was right with her soul.

Memories of Zane's proposal filled her

with a gentle eagerness she'd never felt before. In the past, she had woken up to start each day with a fierce determination to keep the unhappiness and guilt at bay. Now, for the first time since giving Miley up, those thoughts didn't disrupt her morning. Instead, she embraced the happiness she felt and looked forward to what was in store. Before they had gone to their separate rooms the night before, Zane had promised that he wouldn't breathe a word to the girls about their engagement until Liv joined them that morning. And they would tell the girls before they'd tell anyone else.

Liv left the comfort of her bed and quickly changed into a nice outfit. Though she was eager to see the girls and Zane again, she forced herself to take the time to put on a little makeup and to do her hair. It was still early—much earlier than she would have usually woken up after staying awake until after midnight the night before—but there was no way she could sleep with the excitement she felt.

During her morning routine, she put a pot of coffee on and had two mugs of steaming brew in her hands as she walked down the hall to Zane's suite. Her stomach filled with butterflies and she couldn't wipe the smile off her face, even if she had tried. Part of her was afraid the night before had been a dream, but when Zane opened the door for her a moment later, the look on his face told her it was real.

Very real.

"Good morning," he said, his voice gentle and sweet as he took the mugs of coffee from her and set them on the counter in his suite. He put his hand on her stomach and gently nudged her into the hallway, before closing the door behind him. "I need to greet you properly."

Wrapping his arms around her, he pulled her into his embrace and kissed her with the same intensity as the night before.

"Good morning," she said on a breathless laugh when he was done.

"There," he said, kissing her forehead for emphasis, "that's how I want to kiss you every morning for the rest of our lives."

Liv clung to him, not wanting to let him go for even a moment. But she knew they needed to put a little space between them until they told the girls their news.

As Zane opened the door and let her enter ahead of him, a niggle of doubt and worry took root in her heart. He had told her that Miley would be okay with their relationship, but what if he was wrong? What if she didn't like seeing them together, even if she thought she would?

Zane handed her one of the mugs and then took her hand and led her to the couch. The door to the girls' room was still closed as he sat close to her on the couch and didn't let go of her hand, intertwining their fingers, so their palms pressed together.

"Where are the girls?" she couldn't help but whisper.

"They should be out here in a little bit. They woke up about ten minutes ago. I told them I had a surprise for—"

He didn't get to finish his sentence, because the girls' door opened and both of them came out. They were dressed but looked sleepy. Alexis wore a pair of orange pants and a bright blue shirt with a basket of puppies on the front.

Liv let go of Zane's hand and he gave her a questioning look, but she didn't want to surprise the girls without explaining some things to them first. The last thing she wanted was a repeat of what had happened with her mom on Christmas morning.

"Liv!" Miley said as she raced across the room then hugged her.

Alexis smiled, but she didn't give Liv a hug. Instead, she climbed up into Zane's lap and put her head against his chest—and her thumb in her mouth—as she stared at Liv.

Zane quietly took her thumb out.

"Good morning," Liv said to the little girl.

"Morning." Alexis yawned and snuggled closer to her dad. She lifted her thumb to her mouth again.

Zane set his coffee mug down and then took Liv's mug, putting it next to his own. After he was done, he wrapped his arm around Alexis.

Miley sat on the ottoman and faced them. "What's the surprise?"

Liv's heart beat fast as she glanced at Zane. "Do you want to tell them?" she asked him.

"I think you should." He smiled. "After all, you weren't given the chance to share the last bit of news with Miley like you had wanted."

She could have kissed him again, but she held back—at least for now.

Instead, she looked from Alexis to Miley, her love for them overflowing. "I want you both to know something very important."

Miley nodded eagerly.

"I love your daddy very much."

Zane took Liv's hand in his and gently squeezed it.

Both Miley and Alexis looked down at their hands and Miley's eyes grew wide.

"I also love you two very much," Liv said, reaching out to take Miley's hand in her empty one. "And I want us to be a family, if that's what you want."

"A family?" Miley asked. "Like a real-life family?"

"That's the one," Liv said with a chuckle.

"You'll marry Daddy and come and live with us?" Miley asked, standing up and moving a little closer to Liv.

"Yes."

Miley shouted her delight and then fell into Liv's arms. "I'm so happy!"

Liv glanced at Alexis, who offered a shy smile.

"What do you think?" Liv asked her.

"I think yes!" Alexis said with a decisive nod.

Zane met Liv's gaze, his eyes filled with joy. "I think yes, too."

Miley returned to the ottoman before asking dozens of questions and hardly allowing Liv and Zane to answer one before posing another.

Liv laughed while her daughter's exuberance filled the room.

As the storm continued to blow, and the snow piled up around the snug resort lodge,

Liv Butler had never felt happier in her life.
She wouldn't be alone again, because she finally had a family, and it was good.

* * * * *

*If you liked this story from Gabrielle
Meyer, check out her previous
Love Inspired books:*

**A Mother's Secret
Unexpected Christmas Joy
A Home for Her Baby**

*Available now from Love Inspired!
Find more great reads at
www.LoveInspired.com.*

Dear Reader,

The idea for this book was born when I watched *And So They Were Married*, a romantic comedy starring Mary Astor and Melvyn Douglas, released in 1936. It's a delightful story about two people caught in a snowstorm at a ski resort. I was so enamored with the idea, I brainstormed this book, using Liv Butler, who appeared in *A Home for Her Baby*, as the heroine. I'm always delighted when I take a secondary character from one story and realize they have such an amazing past! Even as an author, I'm still surprised from time to time. Lakepoint Lodge and Lake Madeline are works of fiction, but they could easily exist in any number of places in Central Minnesota. I loved bringing this story to life and sharing a bit of my home state with all of you. I hope you enjoyed this Christmas tale.

Blessings,
Gabrielle Meyer

HARLEQUIN SELECTS COLLECTION

19 FREE BOOKS IN ALL!

From Robyn Carr to RaeAnne Thayne to Linda Lael Miller and Sherryl Woods we promise (actually, GUARANTEE!) each author in the Harlequin Selects collection has seen their name on the *New York Times* or *USA TODAY* bestseller lists!

YES! Please send me the **Harlequin Selects Collection**. This collection begins with 3 FREE books and 2 FREE gifts in the first shipment. Along with my 3 free books, I'll also get 4 more books from the Harlequin Selects Collection, which I may either return and owe nothing or keep for the low price of $24.14 U.S./$28.82 CAN. each plus $2.99 U.S./$7.49 CAN. for shipping and handling per shipment*.If I decide to continue, I will get 6 or 7 more books (about once a month for 7 months) but will only need to pay for 4. That means 2 or 3 books in every shipment will be FREE! If I decide to keep the entire collection, I'll have paid for only 32 books because 19 were FREE! I understand that accepting the 3 free books and gifts places me under no obligation to buy anything. I can always return a shipment and cancel at any time. My free books and gifts are mine to keep no matter what I decide.

☐ 262 HCN 5576 ☐ 462 HCN 5576

Name (please print)

Address   Apt. #

City   State/Province   Zip/Postal Code

Mail to the Harlequin Reader Service:
IN U.S.A.: P.O. Box 1341, Buffalo, NY 14240-8531
IN CANADA: P.O. Box 603, Fort Erie, Ontario L2A 5X3